ROCK STAR

STACEY KENNEDY

Stacey Kennedy
www.staceykennedy.com

Edited by Christa Soule
Copy Edited by Chelle Olson, Literally Addicted to Detail
Cover Photograph by Sara Eirew
E-book Cover Design by Charity Hendry
Print Design by Graphic Fantastic

Manufactured in Canada
First Edition June 2017

As always, for my readers.

PROLOGUE

One foot propped against the white railing, Travis Walker pushed the wooden swing back and forth on the porch of his parents' home as he stared out at the quiet, tree-lined street. The day couldn't be any sunnier, with a clear blue sky and only a few clouds, but a heavy darkness hung over the small town of Catfish Creek, Texas.

"It's really happening."

Travis turned toward the soft, sweet voice, finding his high school sweetheart, Rae Evans, sitting next to him. She stared at the *For Sale* sign with the *SOLD* sticker diagonally across the front. Her long, straight, brown hair curtained her face, but he could see the sadness in her pretty hazel eyes. "Yeah," he answered her statement, "the realtor came today, and my parents accepted the buyers' offer."

Even as he said the words, he begged for them not to be true. From this day on, their lives would be forever changed.

When they graduated a couple of weeks ago, a big-time agent from New York showed up with a recording deal. One that would make all of Travis's dreams come true.

"When do you leave?" Rae barely whispered.

"Tomorrow morning," he replied, reaching for her hand and taking it in his, wishing, somehow, he could hold onto her forever. "I'll be staying with my agent while my parents get the house packed up and move into the city."

"That's good," she said with a soft smile that didn't reach her eyes. "You know, that you have a plan and everything."

Travis's heart clenched, and he ran his thumb across the back of her palm, doubting his every move and all the decisions that led him to this moment. His parents always told him not to get too serious with Rae. He was only eighteen years old, as was she. They were too young, too immature, too inexperienced in life to know what they wanted.

His parents were wrong.

He loved Rae with all that he was. Deeply. Madly. Irrevocably.

In the silence that stretched between them, a painful sense of distance seeped into the air. One Travis had never felt before. One that felt so…wrong. One that he wished he could remove with every breath he took.

Obviously, she felt the icy whisper, too since she smiled again, clearly to lighten the mood, and said, "I bet, one day, girls will throw their panties at you."

ROCK STAR

The swing slowed, and he pushed against the railing again, sending them swaying. "Most girlfriends wouldn't want other girls throwing their panties at their boyfriends."

"Well, I don't want that, of course…" She hesitated, lips pursing, then added, "But to be honest, I guess I kinda do."

"And why is that?"

Her eyes sparkled, so full of dreams and life. "Because that would mean you made it. That you became the rock star you always hoped to be. And that everything I hoped and wished *for* you came true."

God. His heart twisted with the misery of how life had brought them to this fork in the road, one where they knew they were about to go off in different directions. "You're not wrong, I guess, even if the logic is a bit warped." He'd never really had the drive she did, but somehow, she always made him want to do better. For her. She forced him, all too naturally, up to her level. "And what about you? What about your dreams?"

"I've got enough AP credits to fast-track through undergrad to veterinary college so I can finish sooner." She pulled up her legs onto the swing, sitting cross-legged. "I figure there's no reason not to dive right in."

"You could live a little," he said, offering her another choice. "Maybe travel?" *Come to New York with me!*

She shook her head. "That's not in my thirty-year plan."

"What is then?"

"Opening two clinics," she replied, glancing at the car driving by and giving whoever was inside a wave before adding, "And to do that, I need to get my schooling over as quickly as I can. So I'll double up on courses and take summer school, too."

What about me? brushed across his subconscious. But he was leaving her, too because he couldn't make music in Catfish Creek. Well, he could, but he wouldn't go anywhere. "It's a good dream," he told her. "And I have no doubt you'll do everything you set out to do."

"I will." There wasn't a hint of insecurity in her voice.

That's what he loved about Rae. She never wavered in the things she wanted, including him. He'd never met anyone who had such clear purpose in life at such a young age, but he knew it was because of her logical mind. Things never got murky or messy for her. Emotions simply weren't part of her internal make-up. Maybe, sometimes, he wished she thought more like him.

The tightness in his chest rose again. Their time was dwindling. What would happen to them? Would she forget him when he moved? Would he forget her? Feeling the icy wisp of dread, he took one of her hands in both of his and kissed the back of it, eyes on her.

Whatever she saw in his expression drew her brows together, and she said, "I want you to promise me something, okay?"

"What's that?"

ROCK STAR

"That no matter what, you will live out your dreams fully and completely." Eyes locked onto his, she added, "I never want to be the one who holds you back."

He drew in a long, deep breath, seeing a new clarity in her he'd never seen before. It made him realize that she knew how hard walking away would be for him, and understood that he had doubts about his choice to leave. "You could come with me," he offered. "Go to school in New York."

She paused, shut her eyes, then reopened them, misty-eyed. "My life is here, my family is here, and so are my friends. I don't ever want to leave Catfish Creek." She placed her feet back onto the porch's whitewashed floor and turned to face him. "If we truly love each other, let's promise to always love each other right—make sure everything we want comes to pass. That we never, ever give up anything of ourselves for the other person. Promise me."

His throat tightened, chest squeezing at the thought of leaving her. She was his everything. "I don't want to leave you."

"But you're only leaving for a little while," she retorted, twining her fingers with his. "We can see each other on weekends. Maybe I can fly to see you. Who knows, once you make something of yourself, maybe you can move back here."

"But…"

"Travis," she said, sternly giving him the *look*, leaving no room for argument. "You do your music. I'll do vet school. If that leads us back to each other, then it's meant to be. I'm sure the romantic in you loves that idea."

He snorted and shook his head. "I don't understand how you can always be so practical."

She shrugged, giving a lopsided grin. "It's both a gift and a curse."

His curse.

On one hand, he agreed with her, they needed to follow their dreams. On the other hand, he hated not choosing love. Deep in his heart, it felt as if he were ripping his soul apart. A part of him would always remain here, with her. "We can't ever take this back, Rae," he said. "Once I go, I'm gone."

"I want you to live your dreams, Travis." She lifted her chin and squeezed his hand, and he could tell she was already decided. "And I want to live mine, too."

CHAPTER 1

Travis Walker made women's panties disappear.

On most nights, anyway.

Tonight, sitting on a wooden stool set upon the stage at Catfish Creek High School's conference center, only one woman was on his mind. His fingers strummed over the strings of the guitar, mouth rested near the microphone, and after he sang the final two lines of the chorus—*I wanna kiss you under the moonlight. And love you 'til the sun comes up*—the applause from the crowd reopened his eyes.

Sparkling string lights and masquerade masks hung from the ceiling above him, reminding him that he wasn't surrounded by thousands of his typical screaming and wild fans. In his Texas hometown, he stared out at teachers, old friends, and classmates, all dressed in formal wear and masquerade masks.

From his seat in the spotlight, he recalled playing for smaller crowds on this very stage back in high school. Those had been some of the happiest days of his life. Now, fresh off his last world tour, he realized he loved that scene, too. The energy of a smaller crowd, who knew him personally, and a larger crowd, who thought they were in love with him, was so different he couldn't compare the two, but admittedly, he missed the intimacy that came from a smaller venue.

Done with his song, and with the crowd quieting, he slid the guitar strap over his head and handed the instrument back to a member of the band that'd been hired to play at Catfish Creek High School's ten-year reunion. When he jumped off the stage, he sighed in relief, finding that all the cell phones pointed in his direction were now put away, and the flashing lights were gone.

That's when he set his focus on what mattered tonight: finding *her*. Rae Evans—the muse behind the song he sang tonight, *Moonlight*.

He scanned the crowd overtop the decorated tables with their gold chairs, but the beauty had escaped him somehow. He recognized Annie Flowers, the librarian, who gave him a little wave, and Christopher Christianson, the principal, who was grabbing a drink from the bar. Travis could have sworn he spotted Rae entering the masquerade ball when he began his song. Desperation now clawed at his chest.

Determined to find her, he moved farther into the crowd, just as his cell vibrated in his pocket. Knowing exactly who it'd be, and that he couldn't ignore the call, he reached for his phone and then frowned at the text from his manager, Scott Price.

Awesome job. The video is already up on YouTube. Fans are loving it. The mask was a nice touch. Don't miss your flight in the a.m.

Travis shifted the black masquerade mask around his eyes, and the muscles along his shoulders tightened with the reminder of the weight they carried; of the need for him to always be on point, and the fact that nothing, not even his high school reunion, was sacred anymore.

Life had changed dramatically since the last time Travis stepped foot in the conference center. But he didn't want to think about the shit weighing on him, so he fired off a response—*I'll be on it*—then tucked his cell phone back into his pocket.

He had tonight to fix everything that was wrong with his life, and he wouldn't waste it.

In the eyes of his manager, Travis had come to the reunion to put on a show and to look *real* to his fans. But Travis hadn't come for the publicity; he had come for one very good reason: to find his anchor—the woman who stopped his world from spinning wildly out of control.

Lately, in a sea of chaos, he'd finally stopped drowning and saw a way back to the happiness he once had. That happiness had started with Rae, and surely, she was his way to find himself again.

One touch. One taste. He wanted to remember what that happiness felt like.

Again, he searched the crowd, ignoring the way some men glowered at him, and some women batted their lashes. *Rae.* That's whom he'd come here to see tonight. Only her.

The band behind him started playing another ballad, and that's when he found her, staring right at him from across the room. She wore a sleek, black, strapless gown around her slender figure with matching long, black gloves.

His muscles surged with adrenaline, and he went to move toward her when a hard voice came from behind him.

"Karly wants you to play another song."

Travis slowly glanced over his shoulder to find the biggest asshole in Catfish Creek High School history, Jason, a blond-haired, slender, one-time big shot. Rae was best friends with Kate, and Kate had loved—and later married and divorced—the dipshit behind him.

Times had changed.

Travis didn't owe Jason anything now, and he certainly didn't owe the reunion's event planner, Karly, shit. "You can tell Karly that I told her I'd play one song, and that's exactly what I did. Bother me again, and we'll have a problem."

Jason didn't make a move or say a word in rebuttal. Once a coward, always a coward.

Refocused on the only person who mattered tonight, and pulled by the energy only Rae conjured, Travis stretched out his fingers, shedding his frustrations as he moved with purpose through the crowd. Her pretty, hazel eyes surrounded by dark makeup followed his every move, and she yanked him forward with a simple look.

She'd always been a pretty girl, but she'd grown into a blindingly beautiful and stunning woman. Her gown fit her like a glove. A gold filigree mask somehow made the creaminess of her skin appear richer. She wore her shoulder-length, brown hair in big waves framing her round face.

Tonight, she didn't look so fresh-faced and innocent. She looked sexy as hell, and just the sight of her again caused Travis's cock to swell eagerly.

While he'd talked to her through email, text, and the occasional late-night, drunk phone call every birthday and Christmas over the last ten years, he hadn't seen her. Not since that day on his parents' porch. Sure, he'd kept an eye on her through the *Catfish Creek Chronicle* when they featured her for her charity work, and also on the website for the vet clinic she owned. But after he'd walked the path that led away from her, he'd never found his way back. Life got busy. New friends were found. Fame overtook him.

Now, he was…*home.*

When he finally reached her, the air between them felt charged. "Rae," he said.

Her eyes warmed. Dark, red-painted lips curved. "Travis."

Christ, he remembered how those lips tasted. How *she* tasted—every goddamn inch of her.

Beneath her mask, those pretty eyes now turned a little suspicious. "Why didn't you tell me you were coming to the reunion?"

Perhaps he should have called, but... "I wanted to surprise you." Because there were important reasons he returned to his hometown, ones that he didn't want her to know about. Yet.

It all began with an article in the *Catfish Creek Chronicle.*

Dr. Rae Evans feels she's done what was needed to help the animals in Catfish Creek, and she's ready to begin a new journey. She's looking to open another clinic in one of the neighboring towns.

At twenty-eight years old, she'd achieved what she hoped to do by thirty, and that article reminded him of the guy he used to be when she'd first made those plans. He wasn't the same man who left Catfish Creek all those years ago, and he didn't know when exactly he lost himself. While Rae had likely found all the happiness she wanted in her success, he simply wanted to find his way back to the carefree guy he once was.

To do that, he had to come back to the place where he was the happiest. He had to come back to *her.* "But to tell you why I wanted to surprise you, I need to tell you a story." He offered his hand. "How about we dance, and I'll share it."

For a second, he thought she might refuse him. She simply stared at his hand.

ROCK STAR

When her eyes met his again, and she slowly slid her palm into his, the tightening in his chest eased. He closed his fingers around hers and sensed her soften, making him smile.

Reliving that infectious energy she carried, he led her into the middle of the dance floor, then he spun her around and pulled her to him, nice and close, sliding his hand across her lower back.

She laughed softly, eyes twinkling behind her mask. "You've still got the moves, I see."

"My moves will never fail me." He grinned.

The band played the perfect song. Something a little sexy and slow, keeping her hips swaying perfectly with his. He did nothing to shield his erection, but one look into her eyes told him that was all right. With her breasts pressed against his chest, her cheeks a little pink now, he noticed the heat in the depths of her gaze. He'd recognize it anywhere. That fire felt like it belonged to him—always had, always would. Yet in the past, she'd shy away from that desire. Now, he noted how she firmly held his gaze, telling him she wasn't the young lover he once had.

"How long are you staying in town?" she asked, in an obvious attempt to divert their attention away from his cock.

"Just tonight." He stroked his thumb over the back of her hand, keeping her as close as he could, inhaling her flowery scent that had faded from his memory. "I fly out bright and early in the morning."

"Only tonight?" She shot him a questioning glance. "You came all the way here from New York just for the reunion?"

"You seem surprised."

She shrugged, seemingly unaffected when another couple bumped into her, her interest obviously centered on him. "Seems like a long way to come for only a few hours."

A very good point, indeed. "Well, you see, that brings us to my story." He sent her out, twirling her around before bringing her in close again and returning the smile she gave him. "But I think we need to go back even further for you to truly understand."

"Go on," she said, watching him closely.

He paused, collecting his thoughts, then he began. "You'll never hear me complain about my life. I have far more than I probably deserve."

"That's a good thing," she said firmly, even as a playful grin teased her lips. "You have a pretty amazing life, and you'd better not complain to me about all the fabulous trips you get to take around the world, or you might lose a tooth."

He chuckled but leaned in, calling her out. "And how do you know so much about my life? Reading up on me?"

"A little," she admitted.

That's what he liked most about Rae. She was honest, through and through. The fact that she followed his life could bite him in the ass later, but at this point, there was no going back, so he pushed the conversation along. "So, then you know that I have a very good life. I travel. I stay in fancy hotels. I eat at amazing restaurants. I never have to lift a finger. I have everything that anyone should want."

Her eyes searched his. "But it's not the life you want?"

Of course, she caught on. He didn't expect otherwise. That's why he'd come to the reunion—to be with someone who truly knew him. "It's not that I don't want the life I live," he explained gently. "It's that something is missing. Something very important."

"Which is?"

"The guy I used to be."

She began nibbling her lip like she used to do in high school when she became confused. "What do you mean?"

"I can have anything I want, Rae. There is nothing that's not available to me." He slid his hand along her spine, pulling her in closer, leaving no room between them. "But the guy I was when we were together…I don't know him anymore."

Her eyes softened, and her voice grew quiet. "That's really kinda sad, Travis."

"It is what it is." He shrugged, not wanting to get stuck on the things he couldn't change. "My manager told me that I'd been invited to the reunion and saw it as a business opportunity. But I saw it as a personal one."

The song shifted to something faster, and the crowd began to fill the dance floor, bumping into his back. He refused to let her go, holding her tightly against him. "Do you want to know the real reason I came to the reunion tonight?"

"Yes," she said, a little breathlessly.

"I came to relive the past, Rae." He released her hand, wrapping his other arm around her and bringing his mouth close to hers. "That's the only reason I'm here. I want to remember what it's like to be with a woman who knows the *real* me." He was encouraged by her shiver. An involuntary movement that spoke of her willingness to give him all that he wanted and more.

Hot and hard, he dropped his head into her neck, inhaled the subtle hints of her flowery perfume, and said into her ear, "We have a chance that many people don't get. To go back and feel what we felt before." He dragged his nose across her neck in the way he knew she liked, feeling her quiver under his hands. "Tomorrow, our lives will return to normal. Nothing will have changed. You'll live here, entirely focused on your clinic and your life, and I'll live mine in New York. Tonight's our one free pass to dip into the past, and I want to take it. Because tonight, Rae"—he brushed his lips across her neck, and a soft moan escaped her mouth as he murmured—"I want one more taste of you."

She gasped and stepped back, blinking rapidly. "I…sorry, excuse me. I need to get some air." Then those pretty pink cheeks and wide, excited eyes were gone, her dress trailing behind her as she ran for the door.

ROCK STAR

Travis shoved his hands into the pockets of his suit and grinned. He didn't mind hunting her, it sweetened his reward.

CHAPTER 2

Rae rushed through the crowd, her chest rising and falling quickly, desperate to get air into her lungs. The conference center's doors were in her sights, and she made a beeline for them. She nearly made it, the handle almost within her reach, when a body sideswiped her. She gasped, latching on to a pair of flailing arms, and soon found herself staring into the fuming eyes of an old classmate, Leah.

Dressed in all black, Leah looked much more badass than Rae remembered from chemistry class.

"Leah, shit, I'm so sorry," Rae wheezed, quickly finding her footing.

"Don't be sorry. I'm not mad at you," was all Leah said before she yanked the door open and vanished from sight, practically blazing a trail of fire behind her.

Rae didn't know what had set Leah off, nor did she plan to

go after her to find out, because Rae burned with an unnatural heat herself.

Not a single man had ever made her feel the way Travis did with just a few simple words or the drag of his nose down her neck. Sure, she'd had other lovers since him. Three of them, in fact, but no one compared to this new, sexy, sensual, confident version of Travis Walker.

Damn it all to hell, tonight's reunion wasn't going as planned at all, and she was reeling, trying to get her head on straight. She'd expected bald men and miserable, divorced women trying to be something they weren't. Not the love of her life propositioning her within a minute of arriving at the damn reunion. She hadn't even considered that he'd be there. Rich and beyond famous now, Travis had outgrown Catfish Creek a long time ago.

Time and space. That's what she needed, and maybe a damn cold shower.

When she finally made it outside, she took in the fresh air, tipping her head back and inhaling deeply. The heat outside, while stifling, was nothing compared to the firestorm he set off in her body. As laughter drew her attention to her left, she found a handful of people smoking. It didn't smell like cigarettes. She looked right, and there was someone puking in the bushes. God, what the community of Catfish Creek would think of this reunion. Especially considering there were two Christian colleges nearby. Though their behavior didn't surprise Rae much. Most kids she knew in high school were so restricted during their youths—as she'd been by her very Christian parents, who still lived in the same house Rae grew up in—they often fought to break free of the constraints often.

She exhaled again and again, slowly trying to control the beat of her heart, rubbing away the goose bumps on her arms. She needed quiet. She needed to think and pull herself together. Travis threw her world into a tailspin. She simply had to realign it.

Determined to do exactly that, she spotted the school ahead of her and made quick work of entering the light brown brick building. The loud doors clanged shut behind her. Lockers lined the hallway, and as Rae strode past, she saw the one that'd been hers: 178. Shockingly enough, it still had the dent in the bottom that had been there ten years before. Even now, she could picture how the inside of the door had been covered with pictures of her squad: Travis and her, her best friends, Kate and Tessa, as well as Jake, Catfish Creek's quarterback and Travis's closest friend.

Her high heels clicked against the shiny floor, echoing in the hallway as she turned and entered through the single door on the left. Immediately, the wonderful scent of dust, paper, and a little bit of mold made everything better. Row after row of bookshelves filled the long, rectangular library, broken up only by the tables scattered throughout.

ROCK STAR

Rae felt her muscles go lax. Some people needed a smoke, or a shot of alcohol, or maybe even a bath to relax. She needed books. They were her escape. She'd spent as much time with books as she did with Travis throughout high school. And even at twenty-eight years old, books were still a big part of her life. She moved to one of the bookshelves and trailed her fingers along the spines. The knowledge within the covers, the stories, the lives lived fully and completely…she relished it all.

"Still predictable, I see."

She whirled around, finding Travis leaning against the doorframe, a big smile on his oval face. Even with the black masquerade mask, and the stylish suit with the skinny black tie, Rae would recognize him anywhere. She recalled in vivid detail how those fingers of his felt when they stroked across her bare skin. How those long legs supporting his thick, six-foot-two frame used to wrap around her after a heavy make-out session. Even how the scruff on his chiseled jaw felt brushing against her inner thighs. Heat flooded her as she swore she could catch hints of his spicy-smelling cologne even from this distance.

She was frozen—unable to move, unable to breathe. She could only stand there as he stared at her, stripping her bare with his warm, gray eyes. That single potent look took her right back to when they were high school sweethearts. When it didn't matter that she had dreams of becoming a veterinarian, and he had dreams of a music career. When life was simpler, and they still had each other.

It was like ten years hadn't passed in the blink of an eye.

But it had.

Hearts were broken.

Lives were changed forever.

She held her breath as he entered the library, and she realized she hadn't answered him. And maybe that was because she didn't want to admit it to herself. If she did, that meant she hadn't changed at all in the last ten years. The old her wouldn't have cared, but now her stomach roiled. "Maybe I am predictable," she said, forcing the words from her throat. "But this is my place, after all."

"It always was your place," he said, nearly reaching her.

Something about his expression changed then as he watched her, becoming a little more intense, a bit more appraising. A swell of heat surged over her just that easily. By the way he watched her, intently, like he was stripping her dress off with a single look, and by the power he exuded, she realized he'd changed a lot in the last ten years, becoming a sensual lover she'd never been introduced to before.

Butterflies danced in her belly as she turned back to the bookcase, trying to avoid him, instead staring at the books she ran her fingers over. "Remember all the times we came in here back in the day?" she asked, recalling some very happy memories.

"Yeah, I do." His soft voice came from behind her, closer now. "We had our first kiss right there at that desk."

She turned and saw Travis gesturing to the table near the outside wall, and she smiled. "We did, didn't we?" Then she pointed to the desk by the window and waggled her eyebrows. "And remember what happened there?"

He glanced at the private workstation near the back of the space and then turned back and grinned at her. "How could I forget? I had a hard-on for the rest of the day."

She laughed and moved all the way to the last bookshelf where the history books were and leaned against the shelf, watching him close in on her. Sweet Jesus, he was gorgeous in a very mysterious and sensual way. All emotion. All passion. That's why she'd fallen in love with him. That's why her heart never forgot him.

"Rae," he said softly in response to whatever look had crossed her face before closing the distance between them.

He cupped her cheek, and she leaned into his touch. "I'm not sure…I'm not sure what you're doing, Travis."

His eyes warmed with emotion as they followed the path of his thumbs, dragging across her parted lips. "I need to feel what it's like to be near you again."

"Why?" she asked, her hands waving at the space around her. "You have everything. You're rich. You're famous. You've got the life you always wanted, and you could have any woman you want."

"You're right, I could." With smoldering eyes, he continued to watch his thumb slide sensually across her bottom lip. "But

I don't want any other woman, Rae. I want you. We have this one night until reality returns and life carries on. Why not relive the past?"

Her mind swam a little. What about *her* did he miss so much? Surely, he'd had far better lovers over the last ten years than her eighteen-year-old self. And why did he feel the need to remember what they had so badly?

She stared into the depths of his eyes, reading the heat in his gaze, feeling like no time had passed at all. Travis had always thought she was the practical one. She had been to make sure they didn't give up their dreams, but there was heartbreak and tears after he left. She was broken for a very long time before she threw herself into her career, forgetting everything else… including her heart.

But now, her heart reminded her of the danger. "I can't have sex with you, Travis."

A smile teased his mouth. "You don't have to have sex with me. That's not why I'm here."

"Then what do you want?" she whispered.

One brow lifted. "I already told you, I want a taste of the past."

Her heart raced at this new Travis. His bold words, the sensual promise in his eyes. The Rae of the past would have never taken such a risk, but maybe she was tired of being so practical and always doing the right thing. It was only one night…what was the harm?

ROCK STAR

She grabbed his tie, pulled him closer. "Then take the taste you want," she heard herself whisper.

He gave a sexy smile, leaned forward, and pressed his lips to hers. At first, his kiss was teasing, slowly reminding her of the guy he was. But then he took over and took charge, changing the osculation into something hotter, something raw and addictive.

She moaned against his strong mouth as his hand slid across her cheek until his fingers threaded into her hair. With a tug, he pressed his lips harder against hers and deepened the kiss. Heat rushed from her head down to her toes just that easily. Goose bumps instantly rose, while he took her into an embrace that reminded her of the passion between them yet hinted at something more. His bold kiss spoke of experience and tasted of longing.

"Tonight's all about you." He backed away and slid his finger across her lips, then down her chin until he reached the top of her sweetheart neckline. "Every goddamn fucking inch of you."

Her heart raced a mile a minute, and she pressed her hands against the spines of the books as Travis gave her a sexy smile and lowered to one knee. He tilted his head back, watching her intently as he gathered up her dress so he could slide his hand up her thigh. She bit her lip, observing him, as his fingers gingerly climbed up her calf.

"So soft and perfect," he murmured. When he reached her inner thigh, she shivered, and his smile grew heated. "Still so sensitive, baby?"

"Yes…God…yes." Her eyes fluttered closed at the new confidence he exuded, a soft moan spilling free as his fingers slid across her sex to move to the other thigh. He played a little, teasing her in ways he never had before. By the time she opened her eyes again, she was trembling in her high heels.

"Do you want me, Rae?" he asked, eyes locked onto hers.

"Yes, so badly."

Never looking away, he slowly inched his hands up. Her chest rose and fell with her heavy breaths. When he finally had her dress up to her hips, revealing her black lace panties, his grin turned wicked.

"Wearing such pretty things. Perhaps you hoped you'd see me tonight."

She couldn't respond. Not now, at the way he looked upon her, and definitely not when those smoldering eyes lifted to hers, and she saw the hunger in his gaze. He licked his lips and kept looking at her while he slid her panties off to the side.

Then he turned his attention to her sex, and she could only watch as he did what he wanted. Boldly, and unabashedly, he stared at her sex. "Fuck, Rae, you're so damn beautiful." She gasped as he flicked his tongue out, gently stroking her lower lips. "Spread your legs for me, baby."

She inched her feet wider, opening herself so he could take her however he wanted. She'd never been this bold, this needy before. But when his tongue expertly flicked along her hot and wet slit, she dug her fingernails into the wood of the bookcase and tilted her head back, enjoying the ride. She remembered how he used to taste her. He'd been a teenage boy then, his skills still raw. Now, he was a man, and she floated in pleasure.

There was nothing hurried about the way he devoured her. He savored every inch of her, and with each slow lick and swirl of his tongue, he drew out her moans. When he tickled her opening with the tip of his finger, she glanced down, seeing his dark head of hair between her legs and his tongue flicking out over her flesh. She threaded her fingers into his hair, holding him to her, and his guttural moan vibrated against her. Then he leaned away and looked up at her, his eyebrows drawn in focus. He bit his sculpted lip as he slid one finger inside her and then another until both were working in a perfect rhythm.

"Don't stop looking at me, Rae," he said softly. "I need to see those eyes."

Doing as told, she watched him, which was no easy feat. His fingers began pumping, the heel of his hand banging against her oversensitive clit. When he swirled his palm over that bundle of nerves, it was all it took to send her crashing over the edge. She shivered and moaned… God, how she moaned when she came, but it wasn't until those noises turned to whimpers that she realized she probably shouldn't have been so loud.

Slowly, she recovered and released her tight grip on the bookshelf, yet he sent her wiggling against his mouth as he licked her slit from back to front, gathering up all that she had to offer. Only then did he right her panties and rise, lowering her dress and pressing the strength of his body against hers.

"Taste what I did to you," was all he said.

She flushed against the brave order. But this game was fun, and she played the seductress, cupping his face and kissing him like she meant it. His tongue swirled with hers, and she tasted herself, scented herself, and it brought on a ravenous hunger to devour him.

When she lowered her hands and reached for his belt, his hand came down on hers. "No," he said, sounding tormented as he pressed his forehead against hers.

"Why won't you let me touch you?" she asked.

He hesitated. "I needed this moment, Rae. Please don't ask why, just give me this."

She heard the desperation in his voice before she saw it in his eyes when he looked at her. Her heart squeezed as she cupped his face, seeing something in him that she'd never seen before. Something dark and troubled. "Travis, what's wrong?"

His brows drew together. "You breathe life back into me, Rae."

Her lips parted to respond when a loud, harsh voice cut in, "You shouldn't be in here."

Rae gasped, dropping her hands by her sides, as Travis glanced sideways. That's when Ballston, aka Ballbuster, the football coach from back in the day, glared at Rae.

"I…I…" She glanced at Travis, looking for help, mirroring the time the coach had caught them making out behind the bleachers before a football game.

Travis gave a bright grin, and she felt the heat rise to her cheeks as he said to Ballston, "I was just enjoying a taste of the past. Is that a problem?"

Ballston frowned and gestured. "Take the party back to the conference center."

Travis grabbed Rae's hand, and in no time, they were out in the hallway again. He looked at her. She looked back. Then, in that free and easy way they had back in high school, they burst out laughing.

CHAPTER 3

The next morning, Rae exited the coffee shop on the corner of Main Street and headed toward her vet clinic, basking in the sunny day. If her feet weren't sore from all the dancing with Travis the night before after they returned to the reunion, she'd think it had been a dream. Hell, the entire night, up until he deposited her in the cab and gave her a final kiss goodbye, watching as the car drove away, seemed like a total fantasy.

"Hey, watch out!"

Rae blinked, snapping out of her thoughts. "Sorry," she called, stopping herself from walking straight into someone on the sidewalk.

She pushed the memories of her unbelievable night away and focused on the street around her, trying to center her world again.

ROCK STAR

Catfish Creek's downtown had changed a lot in the last ten years. It had grown to accommodate new stores and chain restaurants, keeping up with the modern times and an evolving city. But the Hamburger Shack hadn't changed all that much over the years, and likely still had the original paint on the exterior. They also had the best greasy burgers in town, so no one ever cared what the place looked like.

Rae reached one of the original buildings on Main Street, built back in the 1840s. It was now home to her vet clinic, Catfish Creek Animal Hospital, and she was happy she'd kept some of the building's charm. With its commercial, Victorian, iron-front architecture, she hadn't modernized the building too much when she bought the place with the inheritance left to her by her grandmother's estate.

She entered through the front and shut the finicky door behind her, smiling at her receptionist, Sandy Lynn, who waved back since she was talking on the telephone. Dogs barked and cried in the kennel behind her as she made her way down the hallway. She passed the four exam rooms before entering her office on the left.

On her desk, she found the newspaper article the *Catfish Creek Chronicle* had written about her a month ago, telling those in the area that she was steps away from turning her clinic into a chain. In the neighboring city, she'd noticed a big space on the map without an animal hospital. This coming February, she'd turn twenty-nine, and that only gave her a year and change to get her second clinic up and running. She set goals and achieved them. They gave her purpose, and that's why she was as far ahead in her professional life as she was. She'd sacrificed a personal life to soar professionally. But, sometimes, she wondered if she excelled jobwise because she had no personal life to speak of. She wasn't sure she liked that.

Seeing Travis last night only reminded her how much she'd given up to get where she was today. Yes, she was proud of everything she'd accomplished, but she couldn't help but wonder if she'd done the right thing. She didn't feel as happy as she thought she would after reaching her goal.

With a sigh, she dropped down into her leather swivel chair. After a quick sip of her coffee, she placed the paper cup next to her keyboard on her antique, whitewashed desk. While her thoughts were on the busy day ahead of her, and on her next steps for the future, she couldn't help but think about last night. She swore she could still hear Travis's voice, feel his tongue working her expertly. She even remembered—vividly—how his fingers felt thrusting inside her. God. She shivered, recalling the new insane heat he exuded. But something about him last night made her feel cold, even today.

He seemed…troubled, and she couldn't make sense of that. He'd wanted to touch her, but not take anything back for himself. He wanted her to lust over him, crave him even, that much was clear. He wanted her to give herself to him. But only for one night?

ROCK STAR

Why?

Last night, she'd tried twice to get him to take her somewhere else for a little more of the *past,* but he only wanted to dance, talk, and reminisce. He wasn't acting like the boy she remembered or the hot rock star that could get any woman he wanted. He was acting as if *she* were what he came back for, and she couldn't understand it.

Determined to figure it all out, she turned toward her computer and opened her web browser, navigating to his Instagram page. There, she found photos of him and all his traveling. God, she envied that. She also took note of his millions of followers, only reminding her how different they were. Her clinic's Facebook page had maybe 5,000 *Likes,* and she had the most successful vet clinic in Catfish Creek.

Shoving that thought aside, she brought up his band's YouTube channel. Clip after clip, she watched Travis being interviewed by reporters. She watched the videos from early in his career, and in them, he was the guy she remembered. Alive. Vivacious. Clear and determined in his path. But in the more recent ones, he seemed dark…different.

A sudden knock on her door made her lift her head, only to find Travis, wearing a pair of worn blue jeans, a gray T-shirt, and a black cotton vest. All those things screamed *hot*, but it was his black beanie that made him look so damn sexy she barely stopped herself from letting her tongue wag out.

His eyebrow lifted, mouth curved. "Are you watching You-Tube videos of me?"

"Er…" She fumbled for her mouse, desperately attempting to close the tab on her browser. He didn't say anything more, but oh, boy, did he still grin at her.

Nothing about this amused her, nothing at all. "You are *not* supposed to be here," she said so fast she barely heard the words coming from her mouth. "Was your flight delayed?"

He shook his head. "No. I changed my mind about leaving this morning."

She shot up from her desk, grabbed his shirt, tugged him into her office, and then slammed the door shut behind him. "You cannot be here. Last night was last night. You know, for ol' time's sake, but you were leaving. That's what you said," she reminded him. "That you were leaving this morning, and our lives would go back to normal. You staying isn't life going back to normal. The reunion is over. It's time to go home."

And she needed that because last night was so much more than she thought it would be. Eighteen-year-old Travis was hard to forget—not that she ever really had. But this confident version of him tripped her heart in very dangerous ways. And she could not afford to fantasize about a possible future with him. There were too many reasons not to even hope for it. The number one reason was the same as it had been ten years ago—she lived in Catfish Creek, and he lived in New York.

Travis frowned, leaned against the closed door, and shoved his hands into his pockets, looking far too sexy doing something so simple. "Well, I decided that was a terrible idea," he said breezily. "To be perfectly honest, I decided I absolutely needed to see you again. Did you not enjoy yourself last night?"

She rolled her eyes. "Yes, of course, but—"

"Then why don't we explore that *fun* a little more?" His smile was pure sin.

Her mind yelled *go.*

Her heart screamed *stay, no…leave.*

Her body shouted *hell yeah!*

Silence fell, and he glanced around her office and then smiled at her. "I'm really proud of you, Rae. Look at this place. It's amazing."

"Oh, no," she quipped. "You can't just skip over all this. You need to leave. Immediately."

He snorted. "Wow, Rae. Seriously, tell me what you really think."

"Okay, I will," she hastily retorted, pointing at him. "This is bad, and it will lead to nothing good. You need to go. Right now, Travis." She moved to reach for the door handle, and he stepped away as she opened it, her body shaking from the inside out.

This was all too raw. Too real. All the past emotions were simmering right beneath the surface, impossible to ignore. Logic had her telling him to go ten years ago. Things hadn't changed. In fact, their lives were even more complicated now.

He suddenly grabbed her wrist and frowned. "Why is my staying so terrible?"

Because I still love you. Because I live here, and you live somewhere else. Because this can never work out. Instead of exposing her heart and crossing lines she couldn't uncross, she said, "Because that would make what happened last night very complicated." She paused, trying to explain herself clearly.

His eyes searched hers, and slowly he began to smile. "Oh, no you don't," she snapped at his sly expression. "Don't you dare give me that look?"

A little heat rose to his eyes as he stroked his thumb across her wrist. "What look is that?"

"The one that tells me you don't care that this is complicated."

"You're right, I don't care." He tugged her to him, those warm eyes virtually stripping the clothes right off her body. "I decided to stay, and I want to spend more time with you, find out who you are now. But I'd rather do that naked with you beneath me."

She swallowed against the visual in her mind. His new confidence did disastrous things to her libido, including activating it in ways she didn't want to tamp down. "What do you mean, find out who I am now?"

He half shrugged. "You seem different. I don't know"—his eyes searched hers again—"a little unsteady, a bit more reckless, brash even. It's like I'm looking at a whole new you."

She snorted a laugh. "And you got all that from what happened in the library?"

His smile was dangerously full of heat. "I got all that from the way you spread your legs for me and then came against my tongue."

Her mouth fell open, a soft gasp escaping her mouth. His body heat poured into her, his sexy words simmered, and the promise of an even sexier night ahead made her nipples pucker. She licked her lips, watching the way he took his whole bottom lip into his mouth before she lifted her attention to his deep, gorgeous eyes.

He stepped closer again, his spicy-scented cologne swirling around her. "Let me have you, Rae. Fully and completely."

Her heart raced, heat pooling between her thighs. "How long are you staying for?" Damn, she was beginning to justify this, and her mind roared *bad idea* at her. But…those eyes, that smile, that self-assurance…that *heat*…

"I'm afraid I don't know yet," he said, taking the tip of his finger and dragging it from her wrist upwards. He smiled when she shivered. "That depends."

"On?" she rasped.

"You, and how long you let me stay in your bed." He continued dragging his finger up and over her shoulder. When he reached her jawline and began tracing up her cheek, he added, "This isn't really all that complicated, Rae. I want you. You're the only one who…" His desperate whisper trailed off.

He cupped her cheek and stared at her intently, and that's when he opened the barrier between them. She sucked in a deep breath, seeing what he so clearly hid from others. *Misery.* The type of personal agony that takes one's breath away. Loneliness in a busy life full of people. Her heart broke a little. Why was he miserable? What about his life was draining all that incredible energy and spirit from him and leaving him this engulfed in pain?

"What exactly are you asking of me?" She needed this to be clear.

His mouth twitched, and his voice deepened. "There's quite a lot I'd like to request of you." He threaded his fingers into her hair, and her body turned to mush in the tight hold as he added, "But for now, I'd like to take you out tonight to Rebels, would that be all right?"

One more night certainly couldn't hurt…*right?*

Curiosity and intrigue made her decision an easy one. Before deciding if sex was on the table, she needed to find out why a guy like Travis, one who had it all, looked so damn sad. And to do that, she needed more time. "Seven o'clock, okay?"

He nodded. "I'm staying at the hotel around the corner from the bar, so how about I meet you there?"

She inclined her head in agreement, and her breath hitched at the way his mouth curved. While she knew the action would happen seconds before his mouth met hers, the power of the kiss couldn't be anticipated. He put everything into it. His fin-

42

gers clutched her hair, and he cradled her body so perfectly against his. His tongue danced with hers, not roughly to own; but sensually, to invite her.

By the time he backed away, her blood was racing through her veins, and she was breathless. "Tonight," she said.

He smiled. "Tonight."

Meet me at Rebels in an hour if you're still in town."

The unexpected text from Jake, Travis's closest high school friend, had brought Travis to Rebels earlier than he'd planned to meet Rae. Travis hadn't seen Jake at the reunion at all last night, which was weird because the guy had said he'd be there.

When Travis arrived, he found Jake sitting on a stool at the main bar, shoving his hand through his blond hair. His friend looked the same as he did back in high school, athletic enough to play in the NFL. And if he hadn't spectacularly broken his arm senior year, the scar on his right bicep a lasting memory of that tragedy, that probably would've been the case.

Jake wasn't the only thing that hadn't changed much. The rock and roll bar on Main Street looked the same, except for the steel bar stools with black leather seats, and the purple under-table lighting beneath the high tables. The black walls remained, with guitars filling up the bare space. Betty even served up drinks from the bottles of booze lining the shelves behind the bar like no time had passed, though the owner's face showed her age. No one could hide a lifetime of partying.

Travis took a seat next to Jake, and barely had time to catch up with his childhood friend before Betty placed two glasses of whiskey in front of them that neither he nor Jake had asked for.

"Well, then." Travis lifted his half-full glass. Betty had obviously seen what he had. Judging by Jake's deep frown, he needed this drink—and maybe a few more after. "To Betty."

"To Betty."

"I heard that," she called from the back room. "Stop stalling and take your shots. My grandmammy always said men were the weaker sex, and you're bound and determined to prove her right."

Jake chuckled before tossing back the entire drink, though his smile faded just as fast.

Travis laughed, too. As a kid, he would have killed to play a weekend gig here. The closest he ever got was when the bar had all-ages open mic events. In fact, his agent discovered him on one of those nights.

When Jake lowered the empty glass, Travis began to wonder if the reason his friend called him here was the same reason Travis hadn't seen Jake at the reunion last night. He narrowed his focus on his friend and realized he knew exactly why Jake needed to unload. Ghosts lived in Jake's green eyes. "Damn." He whistled softly. "I know that look. You have woman trouble."

"You don't know the half of it," Jake muttered.

"I have some time to talk," Travis said after finishing off the remaining whiskey. "That's why you asked me here, isn't it?"

"This isn't something that can be talked through," Jake explained, voice grim. "I fucked up. Now I just need to figure out how to fix it."

Seeing that his friend searched for a way to forge ahead, Travis rested an elbow on the bar and recalled advice that his father once gave him after a fight he had with Rae. "Word of advice, don't take the safe way out—flowers and chocolates and that shit. Do something that will have special significance to *her*. It'll mean more, and she might stand still long enough for you to get down on your knees and beg for forgiveness."

Jake cleared his throat, finally looking at Travis. "You have a lot of experience with that sort of thing—the getting down on your knees and begging bit?"

Travis smirked. "There's always a first time." At this point in his life, he wanted someone that required that of him. Most women dropped to their knees without ever asking anything of him. It wasn't something that made him proud.

Travis wasn't sure if it was what he'd said or if something had suddenly clicked in Jake's head, but the man cursed and rose then glanced over his shoulder.

Travis waved him off, not needing to get in the way of something obviously important. "Go get your woman." Besides, Rae stood behind Jake, and there wasn't a chance in hell Travis would send her away.

"Look me up next time you're in Dallas," Jake said.

He nodded and smiled. "I always do."

As Jake strode off, a smiling Rae stepped closer. Travis couldn't stop himself from giving her the once-over she deserved. Fuck, she was so damn pretty. She wore a white summer dress with brown cowboy boots, and her hair was perfectly straight, her makeup light and so Rae. There was such a…realness about her; something that he couldn't ever explain, not even to himself. She was just herself. Always. Never trying to be something she wasn't. More importantly, he'd never met someone so comfortable in her own skin. But there was more between them now. As odd as it was, it felt as if the love they once shared was simmering right there beneath the surface, but it had the potential to be even better if only they let it grow.

When he came to the reunion, he'd expected Rae to be the same old girl, the woman who always picked logic over love, but she seemed different. His old Rae would have never let him go down on her in the library. His old Rae would have never changed her mind when he pushed her to let him stay. It was a transformation he couldn't ignore. He needed to explore this new development more to see if maybe the love of his life was ready to forget practicality and choose love instead.

ROCK STAR

As he looked into her pretty eyes again, she asked, "Is Jake okay?"

"Yeah, he'll be all right." Travis looked at the door Jake had left through, knowing that whatever was going on with Jake was some pretty heavy shit, but it also wasn't his business to share. "Come on," he said, smiling back at Rae. "Let's grab a booth."

She smiled in return and followed him to the far corner away from everyone else, exactly as he intended it.

In no time, they were seated and had placed their orders for chicken wings and fries, which was a Rebels' specialty. In traditional style, Betty had their meals set out in front of them before they could even finish their first drink.

"So, tell me about all the excitement in your life," Rae said, raising a chicken wing to her mouth. "You must have some pretty crazy stories."

Travis picked up a wing, too. "Sure, I have some stories, but they're not worth retelling."

"To me, you mean?"

He laughed and nodded. "Especially to you." After he'd taken a bite, he added, "But believe me, Rae, fame isn't all it's cracked up to be."

"Why?" she asked before ripping off a piece of the chicken, leaving sauce on the corner of her mouth.

He grinned. "You eating that is a perfect example. Do you know how long it's been since a woman has done that in front of me?"

She devoured the wing and even sucked the sauce off the bones. "I hope you're not expecting me to be embarrassed about that because it won't happen. I like food. A lot."

He chuckled. "Actually, I like it. I miss it, in fact."

She paused, eyebrows shooting up to her hairline. "You miss watching a woman eat a chicken wing?"

"Yes."

She snorted and grabbed another from the pile. "You are so weird. You know that, right?"

He barked a laugh, watching her practically inhale her meal. "Take that as another example. I can't even remember the last time someone said something negative to me."

She placed her chicken wing down on the plate and frowned at him. "Let me get this straight. I eat like a pig, and I say mean things to you, and you like it?"

"That's right. I fucking love it." He noted the way she watched him then, a little more intensely, obviously thinking thoughts he wished he could hear.

"Is that what the library was all about? Why you wouldn't let me touch you?"

He held her stare. "I wanted to remember what it looked like, what it *was* like, to pleasure a woman who truly wanted me, not Travis the rock star. If you touched me, I'd have gotten lost in my own pleasure, and I wanted to focus on you alone. I wanted that memory."

She quickly looked away, drew in a deep breath, and then hastily switched the subject. "Even if you don't really like the fame, you still love the music?"

"I'll always love the music." He placed the bones down and sucked the sauce off his thumb. He liked the way her eyes heated, and her lips parted as if she couldn't get enough air into her lungs. "The crowd, the energy that happens when I'm on stage. The thrill never gets old."

She smiled softly. "It's what you always wanted. Your dream has come true. That's great, right?"

"Some of my dreams have been realized." Emotion slammed into his chest. She simply didn't know how much he regretted when it came to her. How much he'd fought over the years to somehow find peace in his life. So many times, he wanted to come back for her, but he needed his craft as much as he needed her. Without the music, he was nothing. But slowly, the years without her grew colder and colder. He couldn't quite remember the happy guy he'd been in high school, but being with her now made him feel like he could find him again.

"Travis," she said softly.

He looked at her then, and whatever she saw on his face made her sit back in her seat as worry filled her expression. He knew why; he'd let his guard down. Walls that he had in place so no one could see the real him, and discover how broken he was. "Fake smiles, Rae," he told her, "that's what got me through. Fake laughter during interviews. Even grinning when

I knew the paparazzi was around me. It was always a show, and I was always on point…until I got home. Until the quiet. Until all that was left was me and the reminder that the two loves of my life—music and you—fought to win, and you lost."

She glanced down at her plate, and he watched her take two deep breaths before she whispered, "I can't do this, Travis."

The noise in the bar all seemed to dull as she became his only focus. "What can't you do?" he asked.

"This. Us. Whatever we're doing here." She finally looked at him, emotion raging in her eyes. "I'm sorry, but I can't do this with you. Last night was fine because it was supposed to be a fleeting thing, not emotional, just some sexy fun. Then we'd wake up and return to our normal lives, and it'd all feel like a dream. But what you're saying now…what you're suggesting… it crosses a line I can't cross with you. It took me years to get to a place where I stopped missing you."

"I didn't know that," he barely managed, never having seen it that way. "I thought my leaving was easy for you."

"Easy?" she scoffed. "I was a mess for a really long time, and terribly heartbroken, but I was the strong one, doing the right thing so that you could go after your dreams. I had to be the practical one, so we didn't end up one of those miserable couples living a life we never wanted because we wanted each other. I did that for *us*."

He cringed, recoiling at how cold her words made him feel, before she added, "I know you don't want to hear that, but I…I can't do this with you. Nothing has changed. This can never work between us. In the end, I'm going to be sitting here devastated, watching you walk away from me again."

The sudden beep of her phone had her reaching into her purse. When she looked at the screen, she sighed. "I'm sorry, there's an emergency at work…" She glanced at him, pain in her eyes before she rose. "I have to go."

"Just wait," he called. "Let's talk."

"I can't," she said, slowly shaking her head. "I'm sorry."

He scrambled to say the right thing…do the right thing… but only managed, "Rae, don't go."

Almost as if she were in slow motion, she moved out of the booth and then came to his side. The soft look she gave him, paired with the sweetness in her voice, broke him as she said, "Last night was amazing." His eyes shut as she pressed her warm lips against his cheek. "But today is a reality that I just can't deal with. My heart is on the line here, Travis, and I'm sorry, but I can't let you hurt me just because you want to dip into the past again and remember the guy you used to be."

When he reopened his eyes, she was gone.

CHAPTER 4

Three hours later, after a successful surgery where she'd removed a sock from a chocolate Labrador's stomach, thus saving his life, Rae returned home to Chestnut Village. She'd been home for a little over fifteen minutes, only having the chance to feed her totally spoiled and incredibly fat, ginger-colored tabby, Harry, before a knock sounded. She peeked through the curtain on the thin window next to the front door and found Travis, his head pressed against the slab.

God, she needed her best friends Kate and Tessa. They'd know what to do and how to handle all this. But only she and Travis were there now. She drew in a long, deep breath as her heart wavered, but her mind held firm. "Travis," she said loudly, ensuring he heard her through the closed door, which in this old house was easy since it didn't have an airtight seal. "You can't be here."

ROCK STAR

"I don't want you to let me in," he said through the door. The heaviness in his voice had her turning around and leaning against the wood for support as he continued. "I understand why you can't do this. I don't want to cross any emotional lines that may hurt you. That's not why I'm here."

He paused, and the silence felt like seconds long before he addressed her again. "I'm here because I want you to know that last night, and even today, the few minutes I had with you, have been the best time I've had in a while." His voice blistered. "You're the best thing that ever happened to me, and I want you to know that you deserve the world in any way you'd like it handed to you. That you were, and always will be, the most genuine thing I've ever known." Then she heard silence followed by the creak of the old wooden stairs beneath his feet, telling her he was leaving.

Again…

Forever…

Earlier at Rebels, she'd been able to walk away from him. Even at the reunion, she could leave him. But something about him leaving her changed the game. Her heart pounded, and the panic of him departing sent her into a frenzy. It was the way he needed her, had reached for her. There was just something between them that she couldn't ignore, no matter what her mind told her to do. In that second where he'd laid bare all his emotions, holding nothing back, she was bared alongside him.

She didn't want him to go.

Logic be damned, she spun around and whisked the door open, not even considering all the reasons she shouldn't.

Travis whirled around and stood there, breathless, his chest heaving. She said the only thing she could, and used his line from earlier, turning it back on him, "Don't go."

She couldn't quite recall what happened next. All she knew was that in the seconds since she'd spoken, she'd ended up in his arms, and they were back inside her house with the door closed.

In her small foyer, he spun her, pressing her back to his chest as he began kissing her neck, his hands exploring her until he cupped her breasts, squeezing and massaging. She gasped for breath, barely surviving his intensity, and leaned her head back to rest against his chest, her moans echoing his. He caressed her as if his hands were made for her body, and she liked it. No, she *needed* the ferocity of his touches. She couldn't let him walk away, despite her head screaming at her that it was the right thing to do.

His mouth settled by her ear while he massaged her breasts harder and groaned each time. She shivered. His touches unraveled her. It was like he'd been desperate to feel her, starved for the way her body warmed beneath his hands, and now that he had her, he couldn't stop.

"Travis," she whispered, arching into him, eager for more.

He turned her around to face him, and she caught sight of his face. Eyebrows drawn, mouth parted, eyes smoldering;

one look, and he set off a fire inside her that only he could extinguish. He grunted, apparently equally affected by what he found in her expression, and then he kissed her, stealing her breath. She followed along, keeping up with the way his tongue twirled with hers, opening her mouth at just the right times to let him own her. His hands trailed over her face, her arms, her hips, until he squeezed her bottom, grinding her against him. Only when he received her breathy moan did he gather her in his arms and move them the few steps needed to the entryway table.

There, he rested her bottom against the tabletop and grabbed his shirt, pulling it over his head in that fast way men do. She had one second to look at him. Lean and ripped; his muscles spoke of power and protection, and of *man*. But before she could look further, his lips were on hers again, his tongue brushing across hers, captivating her once more. She moaned breathlessly, as he inched her shirt up until he had it over her head, leaving her in her white bra.

"Christ, Rae…" He moaned, kissing between her breasts, on her stomach, paying attention to her body; not leaving any of her untouched. "How you feel…" He dragged his nose across her shoulder. "The way you taste…" He kissed along her collarbone. "You drive me fucking crazy."

God, the things he said. This wasn't the boy she remembered. This was a man, and she wanted him so badly. She threaded her hands into his hair as he kissed her ribs, her belly button. He trailed his tongue up her side, and she giggled from the tickle. When he lifted his head, she spied his grin before he took her mouth again, owning her with his special brand of addictive passion.

That's why Travis excelled where other men failed. He took his time. He waited for her body to come alive before he dared to remove her pants. He kissed and hesitated. He urged and guided. And by the time he removed her panties, she was soaking wet and more than ready for him.

"Goddamn it," he practically purred, and her eyes rolled back as his fingers slid across her slick heat, slowly dragging her arousal up to her clit, where he played with the little bud. "I like the way you want me, Rae," he added. "The way you need me."

She couldn't wait. Not any longer. His body was so close to hers, his touch… God, she'd wanted him like this for so long… for so many lonely nights when her heart bled for him. She reached for his belt. "Condom?" she asked.

With quick hands, he pulled out his wallet, then grabbed a silver packet before he thrust his pants and boxer briefs down and kicked them away. Once he had the condom free from the wrapper, he said, "Kiss me."

She did, again and again, as she felt him applying the latex over the hard cock resting on her stomach. He sucked on her lips, her tongue, until suddenly he turned her around.

Facing the wall now, she stared at herself in the mirror over the table. A foreign look of desire was there in her dilated pupils, in her puffy, red lips, and in her flushed cheeks. Even to her, she looked blatantly desperate, but she didn't care.

"Take me," she begged.

In the mirror, over her shoulder, Travis's heated eyes burned into hers. Boldly stating he wasn't the eighteen-year-old she remembered, he reached for her leg, placing her knee on the table, opening her up for him. He didn't wait. With his eyes on hers in the mirror, he entered her from behind right to the hilt.

"Fuck," he groaned, tossing his head back.

She lost herself in the pleasure, but she couldn't stop looking at him. The strength of him, and the way he used his whole body to engulf her in passion consumed her. To have him back inside her was everything and so much more. She'd wished for this moment for years. She'd been tormented by it, imagining him thrusting inside her as he did now. And with each slap of his pelvis against her bottom, she felt the walls she'd erected to protect herself crumble. She craved him. All of him.

She moaned, vocalizing the maelstrom that he created inside her. And like he heard her need, he wrapped his arm around her and pressed her back against his chest. In the mirror, she stared at her breasts bouncing, and the way he claimed her so perfectly, somehow making her feel beautiful and sexy all at once.

But then she lost sight of his potent eyes as he dropped his head onto her shoulder in the crook of her neck and murmured, "Give me what I want, baby."

Her eyesight blurred, and then her lids eventually shut against the pleasure. Her loud moans echoed with his, as skin slapped against skin, his hard cock driving up inside her. His warm, sweaty body pressed against her, the strength of his arms around her, and the scent of him swirling in the air drove her higher.

"Oh, yeah, baby," he grunted. "Just like that, Rae. That's what I want."

Her inner muscles squeezed harder, her arousal soaking him more, as he laced his fingers into the back of her hair, thrusting harder, faster now, not relenting until she gave him exactly what he wanted. And that was her body surrendering to the pleasure he provided.

With a final thrust forward and a loud scream, she gave him everything, shuddering and breaking apart around him until she stood there bare and vulnerable, a mess of orgasmic bliss.

His arms held her tightly, and his sweet, soft kiss on her shoulder brought her back to the moment, as he lowered her leg to the floor, pulled out, and then turned her to face him. His condom-covered cock pressed against her stomach as he kissed her, properly and perfectly, devouring the remainder of her whimpers until her climax had fully released her.

Only then did he look at her. She raised her hands to his face, staring at him intently as he lifted her bottom onto the table, hooked one leg under his arm, and entered her in one swift stroke.

"That one was yours," he growled against her mouth. "This one is mine."

Then, there was no thought, no conversation, only loud, throaty moans filling her foyer. Fiery eyes locked onto her, Travis pumped his hips with rapid speed, his pelvis banging perfectly against her clit every time until he found a rhythm that furrowed his brow and intensified his expression. His mouth parted, then pressed against hers as he took what he wanted. Her. Roughly. Passionately.

Until she felt the widening of his cock, which either awakened her climax from before or brought on a new one altogether. And as his groans became louder, his thrusts a little more urgent, she dug her nails into his shoulders, riding the intense wave. She watched the way his eyes widened before they pinched shut, as he stiffened and roared, bucking and jerking his climax, and she soared right along with him, crashing into a mindless space.

Many minutes later, a sudden meow snapped her back into the present, and had Travis glancing down.

"And who's the little voyeur?" he asked.

Rae glanced at her feet and laughed. "That's Harry."

"Well, Harry, let's get one thing straight," Travis said firmly, parting from her and wrapping an arm around her waist to help her off the table. He kept that arm firmly in place, and when he looked at her, his eyes became intense, and his voice grew thick. "Rae is all mine tonight, so your demands will have to wait."

Travis gathered Rae up in his strong arms, and she wrapped her legs around his waist, as he began to carry her up the stairs toward the bedroom. But as Harry meowed, she laughed again, and said, "I think he might disagree with your statement."

Travis grinned. "Too bad for him, the only pussy I care about tonight is yours."

—︎∿︎—

An hour later, standing before the small, ceramic bathroom sink, Travis cupped the brisk water pouring out of the faucet and splashed it onto his face—his only recourse to cool the blistering heat burning within. He blew the water off his lips and glanced up, staring into his gray eyes that even he didn't recognize anymore at times. Beads of water dripped off his hair and nose, and the longer he stared at himself, the more lost he felt.

Torn by all the things he couldn't change, he splashed his face again with the cool water before grabbing the hand towel resting on the round hook and drying off. Just as he returned the towel to its place, his phone vibrated in his pocket. When he pulled it out and looked at the screen, the text from his manager immediately sent his tense mood into a downward spiral.

You weren't on your flight. What's up?

Travis frowned at the text, desperate to shut the world out, giving him a little more time in the past. The present would come back and suffocate him soon enough. He fired off a return text: *I need a couple more days.*

Not waiting for Scott's reply, he muted his phone and tucked it back into his pocket. Some things weren't for his manager to decide. And after coming off a world tour, Travis deserved a weekend off, no matter that he paid Scott a hefty sum to ensure that his schedule was always busy and that his name was always right in front of everyone's face.

With one last look in the mirror, he left the bathroom, finding Rae dressed in black tights and a long, gray shirt that hung off one shoulder. Sitting cross-legged on the end of her bed, she didn't have to say anything. Her soft eyes said it all. "You want answers," he stated.

She nodded. "I think I deserve them, don't you?"

"You do." He took a seat next to her, keeping his feet flat on the hardwood floor, resting his elbows on his thighs. "This is a complicated conversation," he admitted.

"It can't be *that* complicated." She rested her hand on his forearm.

He stared down at the way she comforted him. If only she knew that comfort was exactly what he'd been missing in his life. "There are times I look in the mirror and don't even know who's looking back at me."

"Like, you've changed?"

He nodded, staring down at his bare toes. "I can't even tell you when it happened, more to the point, why it happened. I only know it did. One day, I woke up and felt like I stood in a world I didn't even know anymore."

"But you love your life?"

"I love parts of my life," he gently explained. "I'm mad about the music. I adore the crowds, the energy that gets created when I make music. The rest, I don't love."

She paused, and he looked at her. Only then did she say, "It's the people in your life that're the problem."

Of course, she got him. She always did. "I've got the boys in the band, but they're all married now, did you know that?"

She grinned and winked. "I might have seen that in an article somewhere. And I think you might have drunk dialed me once from your drummer's reception."

He grabbed her thigh and squeezed. "Don't ever be embarrassed that you've been keeping tabs on me."

"God, don't say it like that," she said, giving him a light, playful smack on the arm. "You make me sound like a stalker. Can we get back to the point please?"

"The point is," he said back, "that the tours are great. It's everything I hoped it would be. Everything we used to sit and talk about. It's amazing, Rae. If only you could see it the way I do."

"I did see it, actually," she said with a soft smile.

News to him. "When?"

"A year ago, in Dallas," she replied. "I was there for a conference, and some of the girls had an extra ticket to your show, so I went." Her eyes twinkled, pride in their depths. "You were amazing. God, I was so proud of you that night."

He recalled the show. He also knew he'd not seen her there. "Why didn't you text me that you were coming? Or come see me backstage?"

She shrugged, picking lint off her tights and flicking it to the floor. "I didn't know if you had a girlfriend, and how weird would that have been?"

"I suppose, for you, very weird," he admitted, though there'd been no girlfriend. But it wouldn't have been weird for him. He wondered what would have happened between them if she'd come to see him. What would he have done?

All the *what ifs* over his life were beginning to drive him mad.

Her eyes searched his, and then she drew in a deep breath, clearly resolving something in her mind. "So back to the stuff before, that's what all this is about, why you came back and want to spend so much time with me? It's to remind you of what your old life was like?"

"Simply put, yes," he said, "but again, it's a lot more complicated than that." He wanted her to understand, so he stuck to the simple version. "You don't know what it's like, Rae. I'm surrounded by people who will give me anything. All the time. I ask a question, and they tell me what I want to hear. So, when I heard about the reunion, I got this idea in my head that if I came back, I'd remember what it feels like to be around people who aren't like that."

The complicated version was that he wanted to see if the happiness he thought he'd felt in the past was real or an exaggerated memory. This weekend with her, he wholly believed his memories didn't fail him.

"But," he added, not wanting to get too far ahead of himself. He raised a hand to her cheek and stroked her soft skin. "I don't want to hurt you in the process of selfishly taking what I need."

She paused. "Okay, before we get into that, answer me this." She stared at him hard. "Do you feel lost, is that what you're saying?"

"I feel like I'm scrambling lately," he admitted.

"Sometimes drowning?"

"Many times, drowning." He sighed. "It feels like I'm this guy that everyone thinks they know. They've got me all figured out in the interviews. They know everything about me, the type of girl I should date, all these personal things about me, and yet…I don't even know those things about myself."

"And you thought coming back here would help you find yourself again?"

"I thought coming back here would remind me of the guy who wanted the fame to begin with."

"That actually makes a lot of sense, and I'm sorry that somewhere along the way things got messy for you." She gave him a sweet smile. "I remember that guy before all the fame. I still see him, but I see something better, too."

"What do you see?" he asked.

"I see confidence," she explained, taking his hand. "But I see sadness, and if spending time with me will make you feel better, then, of course, I'll be here for you."

He couldn't waver, feeling bad enough that he'd shown up at her doorstep instead of leaving when he should have...*again*. "Will I hurt you, Rae?"

Her eyes searched his again before she placed her hand over his on her cheek. "No, Travis, you won't. It was my decision to open the door and let you into my house. We have this weekend. Let's enjoy it."

"Are you sure?"

She smiled and nodded. "I'm sure. We aren't the people we used to be, and I think I simply needed to see that. If you need some time with me to find your way back to yourself, I'll be there for you, Travis, however you need me."

Which told him she likely saw how broken he was, and perhaps the danger of loving him again wasn't so easy. But he needed her, so the rest didn't matter right now. Because he knew he'd picked his career over love all those years ago, and he picked wrong.

CHAPTER 5

The next morning, Rae stirred from sleep with the sun beaming on her face. Though it was Harry who purred loudly in her ear that got her moving. "Yes, I'll feed you," she told the cat, glancing at him as he began kneading the top of her head while he shared her pillow.

His responding sharp meow told her she wasn't moving fast enough.

Even her stomach rumbled, making her aware of all the energy she'd used up last night that obviously needed replenishing. She noted that the clock on the antique nightstand read eight o'clock in the morning, and she debated shutting her eyes and going back to sleep. It was Sunday, after all. But then she remembered that she wasn't alone in her bed, and a different kind hunger consumed her.

She turned, expecting to find Travis sleeping soundly next to her. Instead, she discovered a note written in his handwriting.

ROCK STAR

Gone to Main Street for donuts and coffee.
Be back soon.
−T

She grabbed the note and smiled, running her fingers across the black ink. Just the idea of fresh donuts made her stomach rumble loudly, and the thought of hot coffee didn't hurt either. She sat up in bed, wearing her T-shirt and nothing else from the night before, noticing she was sore in all the right places. Either Travis's sexual appetite had grown over the years, or he had missed her as much as she missed him because it had taken all night before their passion cooled and sleep won out.

Harry meowed again, and Rae reached out and stroked his soft fur, hearing the rumble of his purring from where she sat. He climbed onto her lap, not caring one bit when she cringed as his claws dug into her leg. But the longer she sat there petting Harry, the more she questioned what in the hell she was doing.

Last night at the restaurant, she had had her head on straight and knew indulging in this thing with Travis wouldn't end well. Wasn't going back into the past always a bad idea?

Though one look into those bedroom eyes of his, with all that emotion and the memories between them, and it was like her head couldn't possibly shut out her heart. Travis was hurting, and he needed her to find a part of himself again. How could she refuse him and turn him away?

She sighed, petting Harry's tail. "So, now what do I do, Harry?"

He meowed back.

Knowing there was only one thing to do in this situation, she reached for her phone on the end table and dialed Kate. When the call went straight to voicemail, she dialed Tessa. The three of them had been the inseparable trio in high school, even sometimes dressing the same, and right now, she needed a big dose of girl talk.

Tessa answered on the third ring. "Seriously, Rae. It's Sunday. Do you never sleep in?"

"I'm sorry for calling so early," Rae said, quickly apologizing for the early wake-up, "but it's an emergency."

"That doesn't sound good. What's wrong?"

"I slept with Travis."

"You did *what*?" Tessa apparently dropped the phone, and Rae leaned away to avoid the rustling but placed the cell back to her ear when she heard Tessa say, "Okay, wait... Jesus, I wasn't expecting you to say that. I'm wide-awake now. When did this happen?"

"Last night, but we also..." She dropped her head into her hand and muttered, "Something happened at the reunion, too."

Tessa paused, and soon, her soft chuckle filled the phone line. "I wondered where you'd run off to."

Rae's head hurt just thinking about all this. She'd opened a door she had no intention of walking through, and now there was no going back. "Have I made a horrible mistake?"

"You slept with a totally hot guy who you were madly in love with, and let's not forget he's now a famous rock star," Tessa quipped. "Honestly, why do you sound like someone died? Isn't this a good thing?"

"That's the question, isn't it?"

"Okay, good or not, I'm actually surprised he's still in town. Did he say when he was leaving?"

"No, he never said." Harry meowed again and rubbed his head against Rae's arm, demanding to be petted. She sighed and scratched him behind his ears, adding, "And to be honest, I'm not even sure if he knows the answer to that question."

Tessa paused. "Well, if you ask me, it doesn't sound overly complicated. Enjoy him while you can, and then send him on his way."

But was it that easy? Rae didn't know. Last night, for a split moment when he talked to her, she'd thought she had this all under control. He was different now. She was different. There was no way this could get complicated, but then there'd been the hours spent holding each other, talking, and laughing. It felt like nothing had changed between them at all. "It just doesn't feel like a one-night stand, you know." She'd had one of those before, and Travis could never be something that meaningless.

"You do have a lot of history together," Tessa agreed. "But have things changed for him or something? I mean, he lives in New York now."

"He's not planning to move back to Catfish Creek if that's what you mean."

"Well, then, there is your answer, right?" Tessa asked, like all this suddenly made total sense. "You are both in the same position you were after high school. He doesn't want to live in Catfish Creek, and you do. So, you really only have two choices here."

"Which are?"

"Get on board with having sex for this weekend and enjoying the hell out of it, or put a stop to this. You know yourself best, Rae. What does your heart tell you to do?"

"That's just it," Rae explained. "My heart doesn't know what in the hell it wants. One second, I walked away. The next, I'm having sex with him in my foyer."

Tessa laughed. "How does that even happen?"

"If I knew, then I wouldn't be in this situation." And that's where things got confusing. Rae could have *just sex* with Travis. But this, the way he was acting with her, didn't feel like *just sex*. It felt like more. It felt like there were emotional strings tying her to him. Hell, it even felt like he had no intention of leaving. But maybe that was her past hope creeping up, that somehow they could make it work.

God, what a mess. "I had it all figured out, Tessa. I told myself that I couldn't dip back into the past because of the danger it put me in. Then he showed up at my house, and I don't know, I broke, standing there in front of him. It was like I…*needed* him in ways I haven't needed anybody, all because he bared himself to me. Emotionally. Does that make any sense?"

"Actually, it makes total sense," Tessa said softly as if she totally understood. "Listen, I'm no expert here when it comes to love, but you guys had a good thing back in the day. Maybe it's time to have another good thing, even if it's only for a little while. Who knows, perhaps you can finally get closure for the past?"

"There is that," Rae said, beginning to swipe her hand over Harry's back, as he purred louder now. "This could just be another blip in time that I'll look back on and say…'oh, that's why that happened,' and then it will all make sense to me."

"Totally," Tessa agreed, and Rae could hear the smile in Tessa's voice. "And if it doesn't make sense and you become a total wreck, you'll call me, right?"

"Yeah, I will."

"Good. I'm glad." There was rustling again, and Rae could swear she heard another voice through the phone line right before Tessa asked, "By the way, and sorry for changing subjects, but have you heard from Kate at all? I keep calling her, but she's not answering."

"No." Rae slid her hand over Harry's back until she cupped his tail. "I called her before you so we could do a three-way call but she's not answering."

"Weird," Tessa said.

"Very weird," Rae agreed, watching as Harry flopped onto his back. She began scratching his belly and said, "Listen, before I go and figure out what in the hell I'm doing, how are things with you?"

"Well, it's been..." Tessa heaved a long sigh. "I think Bennett"—Tessa's ex-boyfriend—"is the one who's been harassing me for the last two weeks."

"Seriously? You're still having trouble?" Rae hadn't known, and suddenly, she felt awful for being so wrapped up in herself that she hadn't asked about Tessa's life right away. Because her situation with Travis wasn't dangerous like Tessa's was. Recently, her house had been broken into, but nothing had been taken. Her wallet had been stolen from her purse out of her grocery cart. Thinking on all of that, Rae ignored her pesky cat, worried for her friend. "What makes you think it's Bennett?"

"He's the only one who has a grudge against me," Tessa explained and then gave a long sigh. "See, the thing is, and I didn't mention it before, but I also had a small scare in the restroom at the masquerade ball. Guess who was there? That's right, Bennett."

Rae couldn't even imagine. "God, Tessa, be careful, this sounds really scary. What can I do to help?"

"Nothing right now." Tessa hesitated, and then laughed softly. "I think I've got this covered, but if I need help, I'll call. Promise."

"Okay, I'm glad," Rae said. "And, seriously, next time you have news like this, you should start our conversation with that. Then I would've realized how stupid I'm being hesitating over the best sex of my life."

Tessa laughed. "He's that good?"

"Dear Lord, Tessa, he's a fucking fantasy come true."

"Is that so?"

Rae snapped her head up, and then it was her turn to drop her phone, her face burning hot. "I… You…" She grabbed her cell off her bed and gasped, "Tessa, thanks for the chat, but I gotta go." She ended the call, hearing Tessa laughing in the background.

"So," Travis drawled, stepping into the bedroom holding the tray of paper coffee cups and the bag of donuts. "I'm a fucking fantasy come true, huh?"

She stared into his playful eyes and became lost…that easily. For all the panic, all the worries and concerns a second ago, suddenly, she had none. Because the truth was, she was tired of always being someone who had to be strong and figure everything out. For once, she wanted to shut her mind down and let her heart lead the way.

And her heart and body wanted more of him. "When you look like *that* and come bearing donuts, yes," she said.

Travis barked a laugh, and she loved the way his eyes warmed. "Passed over for donuts. There goes the fantasy."

She grinned. "But they are warm and sugary."

"I'm warm, and hell, am I not a little sweet, too?" He smiled back, entering the bedroom and placing the donuts on the nightstand.

She rose onto her knees as he reached her, and just as his lips nearly touched hers, she whispered, "Give me a little sugar then and let me find out."

One hand in her hair, the other on her cheek, his tongue slid oh-so-perfectly across hers. The power of his touch branded her, raising a flurry of heat within.

When he backed away, one brow was arched. "Well?"

"You're right," she all but purred. "You're better."

―᠎᠎∞―

Later that night, after spending the day in and out of bed with Rae, Travis pulled his rented 1970s Ford truck—the same type of vehicle he'd had back in high school—up to the main gates of the Mustang Drive-In, or the Must-Bang Drive-In as it'd been called back in the day. He couldn't remember a day like he had today. Doing nothing with someone, and yet it felt like everything. The coldness that had invaded him lately slowly began to thaw. She did that to him. It was all Rae. Her warmth.

At the fork in the road, either heading down to the rows of vehicles waiting for the movie to start or going right toward the concession stand, he took a left, traveling up the thin road toward what used to be *their spot* every Friday night.

ROCK STAR

Up on a small hill were two big shade trees, and in between those trees, was the perfect place to not only watch the movie on the big screen in the middle of the field, but also a clearing private enough to handle their teenage hormones.

Sitting next to him on the bench seat, Rae leaned forward and glanced out the window and smiled. "I can't believe our spot is still here."

"I can't believe the Must-Bang Drive-In is still here," he said, pulling in between the trees and putting the truck into park.

"It's crazy, right?" Rae laughed and exited the truck.

As he'd done so many times when they were younger, he grabbed the blanket next to him and joined her outside. At the back of the truck, he found her looking as sexy as ever in a short, lacy, soft pink dress and ballet shoes that had ribbons that tied up her legs. He doubted he'd be able to keep from looking at those legs all night. He dropped the tailgate and asked her, "Does Rhonda Little still own the place?"

"I think so, yeah," Rae said, helping him settle the blanket into place on the tailgate.

"It's so strange, you know?" He held her by the waist and hoisted her onto the back of the truck, her legs dangling.

"What's strange?" she asked.

The truck bounced under his weight when he sat next to her. "How so many things have changed, and yet…how things are still the same. I gotta say, it makes it easier to come back and remember who you were and where you came from when everything you left behind is all still here."

"That's so very true." She gave him a sweet smile, and likely unaware of how damn sexy he found her lacy shoes, swung her legs back and forth, tempting him to wrap those legs around his shoulders. "So, can I ask you a question you might not want to answer?"

He blinked, glancing back into her eyes. "Of course."

"Okay, so…"—she watched him carefully—"you said the guys in the band are married, but why aren't you? I can only imagine you've had a line of women holding out their hands, waiting for a ring."

He chortled. "Is that what you really think?"

"You're quite the catch." She grinned.

"I'm glad you think so," he replied, taking up her hand, hoping what he said next wouldn't shock her too much. "But to be perfectly honest, I haven't had a serious relationship since you."

Her brows shot up. "Never. Not once?"

"Never. Not once," he confirmed.

The music and laughter from the crowd awaiting the movie began to drift up, as her eyes searched his. She finally asked, "Care to explain why you haven't dated seriously?"

He wondered how she'd read into his admission. But he knew the woman next to him, and he also knew she'd need all the answers before she formed any opinions. "You know at first, things were…" He stopped where his thoughts were about to take him and smiled at her, sliding his fingers across her bare thigh beneath her dress. "Are you sure you want to hear this?"

"Yes, I want to know," she said with a laugh and waved him on. "Go on, just spare me the intimate details."

That was easy to do. He drew in a deep breath to gather his thoughts. "All right," he said, hoping he wouldn't regret this. "When everything started happening for the band and me, things were very casual with women."

"So, you fully lived the rock-and-roll lifestyle, drinking into the morning and banging anything that walked into the night?"

He chuckled and shook his head, sliding his thumb across the back of her hand. "I can always count on you to tell it like it is."

Even if that bit of truth put him in a terrible light, he carefully looked for any hint of unhappiness from Rae but found none. Always the supporter, she'd likely only see the good in him at all times. Because that was Rae.

"Well, did I get it right?" she asked, swinging those sexy legs in front of her again.

"Something like that," he agreed gently, forcing himself to look into her pretty eyes. "But the thrill of women and parties and all of it got old really fast. You know, there were times I'd go to sleep in my bed and wake up beside a woman, having no idea how she got there. I didn't know if we'd slept together or not."

She nibbled her lips and then shrugged. "I wouldn't feel torn up about it; they wanted to be there."

"They did, you're right," he said in full agreement, hanging his head, staring down at her fingers twined with his. "That's when I realized there was something worse than waking up and not knowing them."

"What's that?"

He glanced up at her. "Waking up and realizing they didn't care about what happened the next day anyway. All they wanted was that night. The glory and the ability to tell their friends we had fucked. I was nothing more than a popularity contest amongst the groupies."

Classic Rae, she began smiling at him. "If you want me to feel bad for you because you got amazing sex with random women—"

"I never said it was amazing." The louder music now drew his attention, and he glanced out, seeing the screen come to life, illuminating the dark field, showing how many vehicles were there tonight.

She let the silence stretch out between them only for a minute before she guided the conversation along again. "I take it then that one-night stands were eventually something you didn't want anymore?"

"That's right," he said, turning to her again, and the light from the screen showed the soft look in her eyes. That's what he liked about Rae. She never let him throw a pity party long, but she'd happily pull him out of the darkness with her warmth.

"Okay," she continued, tucking her hair behind her ear, "if one-night stands didn't work out, then why not start dating?"

"I tried, and failed."

"Why?"

Because I should be with you, his heart roared. Though it wasn't that simple either. Because for her to be with him, she'd have to give up a lot. But he'd seen the article that stated she had nearly reached her goals, and he wondered if maybe she was ready to move on from Catfish Creek. That's what had brought him home.

But there were other reasons he could never forget her, not even ten years later. She gave him something no other woman had. "When I went on dates, all they saw was the rock star, not Travis Walker. They wanted the show. They wanted the party. They expected fancy dinners and extravagance. They hungered for the tabloids. But no one, not a single woman, ever went past two dates because they weren't with me for the right reasons."

Emotion filled her face at the realization of everything he wasn't saying. She inhaled deeply and looked out in front of her, staring at the movie screen. "I do know what you mean," she eventually said. "I tried dating, too, and it didn't go so well either."

"I can't see how that's possible." She was perfection.

She laughed softly at the compliment. Never able to receive them well, she looked at him with shy eyes. "It's hard to explain, but the guys I met, they just weren't…enough."

"Enough?"

"Enough passion. Enough soul. Enough heart." She glanced down at her legs. "I don't know how else to explain it than to say, they just weren't *enough*. I tried, especially with my last boyfriend because my mom was getting on my case about being single. But in the end, boredom set in, and that was that." She raised her head and gave a little shrug. "We can't be good at everything I suppose, and we nailed our professional dreams."

"We did," he agreed.

But his professional life hadn't been on his mind lately. He wanted more, and he wanted to find his way back to the happiness he once had. He couldn't help but think that *more* rested with the woman next to him. Christ, he didn't have it figured out, but being back here, with Rae, everything felt…right.

"And yet," she said, drawing him out of his thoughts, "do you ever wonder if something's missing?"

Now it was his turn to dig a little into her life, especially considering this topic interested him greatly. "What could be missing from your life?"

"I don't know exactly." She sighed and leaned back, resting on both hands behind her on the blanket, then glanced up at the starry sky. "It's like I planned my entire life, and it all unfolded exactly as I wanted it to."

He stared at the long line of her neck, at the way her hair hung down, of the way she arched her back, pushing her breasts out. "Why do you make it sound like that's a bad thing?"

"Because I'm starting to wonder if it *is* a bad thing. Here I am, just about to reach my thirty-year goals at the age of twenty-eight. I should be happy, thrilled, feel fulfilled."

"And yet…?"

Head still tilted back, she looked at him. "Should life be so planned?"

"For Rae Evans, yes," he replied with a smile. "Remember when you used to plan our weekends down to the hour?"

She laughed quietly, glancing back up at the stars above her. "I still have an hourly planner with sticky notes, and I'm pretty sure I couldn't live without it." Her smile began to fade. "But here I am with everything I wanted. I have a house, a successful clinic, and no debt to speak of, but…"

"Something's missing?"

"Something's missing." She looked at him and gave a tight smile. "I guess I didn't realize just how much until the reunion."

He let that truth settle between them as he glanced out at the movie that now played on the screen. It seemed like he was searching for a way backward, and Rae searched for a way forward. But he wondered if they would still end up in that same spot as before, somehow never able to come together the way they should.

Down below them, most people sat in their cars, but some were like him and Rae, sitting on the backs of their trucks.

Memories bombarded him, good memories. Times when things were a lot less complicated but still emotionally messy.

As the movie played on, he thought Rae might stay quiet and watch in silence as she used to do, but she surprised him.

"Do you ever miss what we had?" she asked gently. When he turned to her, he lost his breath at the emotion in her eyes. "Not who you were back then. But what we had together? What that kind of love felt like?"

He reached up and touched her face, needing to get closer. When she looked at him like that with such feeling, it destroyed him. "Yeah, I miss us," he said, taking her hand into his.

She shut her eyes and leaned into his touch. "If only we could freeze time."

He slid his thumb across her soft cheek, then, unable to stop himself, he caressed her bottom lip. "If only…"

Her eyes opened, heat in their depths. "I want you, Travis."

Christ, he didn't even recognize this Rae, and it fucked with his head. She'd always been so shy, so quiet, so perfect… and yet, he preferred her like this. He'd loved her as a girl. He'd ravish her as a woman.

"What do you want from me?" He pressed harder against her bottom lip, watching intently as her mouth parted, a breathy moan escaping.

She leaned closer to him, her lips right *there,* and whispered exactly what he needed to hear, "Take me like you did that night." She flicked her tongue out, connecting with his thumb.

"What night?" he growled, ready to give her whatever she wanted.

"The night before you left."

CHAPTER 6

With stars spattering the sky above her, Rae followed Travis as he led her to the inside of the truck, his gaze following her with each step he took backward. He moved in the same manner that he had that night ten years ago. It'd been here, right as the movie started, that he told Rae that he was moving to New York to pursue his dream. There'd been laughter and joy. There'd been tears. But there'd also been so much more. Something that had affected her in ways she couldn't have imagined. The way he'd touched her that night and the way he looked at her were imprinted on her mind. That was the look, the *feeling* she'd measured every man against since—and was why she remained single.

No one compared. Not a single man. No one ever cared about her like Travis had.

Once he reached the truck's door, he smiled. "Just like before?"

"Just like before," she whispered, feeling the heat rising within.

His playful smile remained as he dropped to one knee, and the light from the truck spilled out into the night. With his heated eyes on her, he slowly ran his hands up her bare legs, dragging the heat of his touch upwards. "Is this what you remember?" He tucked his fingers into her panties and pulled them down. "Me, touching you like this?"

She nodded and shivered as Travis turned on the switch and focused all his blisteringly hot attention on her. She stepped out of her panties and said, "You look different now."

"How so?" he asked softly.

"Stronger. Sexier."

The lust in his eyes stole her breath. The promise in their depths doused her in need.

"Ah, baby, I like when you look at me like that." He rose and stepped closer, his hard chest to her soft breasts. "Because I want you just as much." He pressed his hand against her back, pulling her to him. "Every kiss. Every touch. Every moan you ever gave to me. It's all there in my mind, Rae."

She gave a breathy gasp as his hard cock pressed against her belly, and her chest rose and fell in anticipation. He slid a hand across her cheek and licked his lips, brushing his thumb across the soft flesh before he sealed his mouth across hers. His kiss held the same desperation she'd sensed back then. The desire to keep hold of something, but the reality that he had to let it go.

His mouth was firm, his tongue was hot, slowly stroking hers, making her ache to feel that tongue between her thighs, and she grabbed his shirt, desperately needing to get closer.

His chuckle shivered across her. "Can't wait?"

"Don't make me," she breathed.

He leaned away, once again dragging his thumb across her bottom lip. Eyes on her, he watched her, and she watched him right back, any barriers between them now gone, only their lustful intentions between them now.

The voices from the movie carried over the hot, dry air, but she's wasn't thinking about the film. She was only thinking of him. She wasn't exactly sure what it was about that night before he left that had made their sex so incredible. Maybe it was the intensity they'd felt knowing he was leaving, or maybe it was something else entirely.

He climbed onto the bench seat in his truck, pulling her up to straddle his waist, and that's when she wondered if it was the tightness of the space that made this so intense, so intimate. There was nowhere else to look but right at him. They were as close as they could possibly get, with nothing between them, not even their secrets. They'd bared it all to each other a long time ago.

Sitting atop him, she reached over and shut the door, the voices outside turning muffled now. The light from the movie glowed through the back windshield as she cupped his face and brought her mouth to his. The odd, unexplainable attraction between them created energy she couldn't control. The same chemistry she'd sought to find with someone else and simply couldn't.

Below her, and between her thighs, she felt his fingers un-hooking his belt. She rose on her knees, getting out of his way and angling her head against the roof. His lips continued their dance against hers as he pushed his jeans down to his knees. Growing more and more impatient, she sucked on his tongue and bit his bottom lip. She was already so wet and warm, eager to have him.

He gave a guttural moan, urging her on, and she slid her lips to his neck, slowly swirling her tongue up his salty flesh, nibbling on his ear the way he used to like. When he groaned deeply, she used her teeth to bite the sensitive flesh.

"Baby girl…" His throaty moan clenched her sex, as one of his hands cupped her nape, pressing her against him, telling her he wanted more of her mouth.

While she was changing the game, doing something she hadn't done that night ten years ago in the truck, she slid off his lap and gave him a quick smile before she glanced down. His cock jutted rock-hard before her, awaiting her. "This needs to go," she said, reaching for his shirt. He had it off a second later, and she began tracing her hands over his chest and down his six-pack abs until she reached the V where she found his erect dick. She grabbed him and stroked, and then she took him into her mouth, right to the hilt.

"Damn," he drawled, stiffening beneath her.

She peeked up at him, finding his head back against the headrest, eyes closed. Determined to please him in the same way he'd pleased her, she got right to it. She slid her mouth up and down over his shaft, her hand following behind. Sometimes, she licked him. Other times, she stroked him. But she didn't stop, she kept going, working him over, tasting him, pleasuring him. The sucking noises began to mix with his moans, while his hand came to the top of her head.

His fingers tightened in her hair, his fist growing tighter and tighter until, suddenly, he grabbed her head, stopping her. "That's not how that night ended," he said with a laugh, taking her arms and moving her back to straddle him.

"Not a bad way to end the night, however." She smirked.

"The most incredible way to end, I'm sure, but that's not what you wanted." He reached between them now, his fingers stroking her wet sex, focusing only on her hot slit for a moment before he concentrated on her clit, working the little bud with swirls of his finger until she gasped in desperation against his mouth, quivering with the tickling pleasure.

His fingers worked back up her body and threaded into her hair, and she gasped as he fisted his hand, locking onto her. He angled her head so that he could whisper throatily in her ear, "Give me something pretty to look at, Rae."

She shivered, never hearing that line before. The younger version of him would have never been so bold. She backed away, watching him grab his wallet off the seat beside him as he took out a condom. While he opened the wrapper, she kept her eyes on him and reached up and pulled the front of her summer dress down, exposing her breasts, showing herself off to him in a bold way that the younger version of her would have been too embarrassed to do.

Not anymore. She squeezed her breasts and played with her nipples, moaning with each and every tug.

Heat infused his eyes as he watched her. No, as he *studied* her, while he rolled the condom onto his hard cock. With a growl that sounded more animal than human, his hands were threaded into her hair again, his eyes gazing deeply into hers, nothing between them. "Do you have any idea how fucking beautiful you are?"

She smiled. "Do you have any idea how sweet you are?"

"I mean it, Rae." He backed away, leaning his head against the headrest, watching her tweak her nipples. "I've been around the world and back again"—he lifted a hand to the curve of her breast and squeezed, massaging underneath while she played and shivered—"but I've never seen anything as beautiful as what I'm looking at right now."

She parted her lips to respond, but his lips sealing over her taut nipple stole the words. He swirled his tongue around the bud before sucking it deep into the roof of his mouth, over and over again, until she was left gasping and wiggling against him.

That's when she found *him*.

The tip of his cock pressed against her slit, and she didn't wait, she slid down onto him, taking him in deep. Their low moans filled the truck as she began slowly working over him, up and down, taking him in as deep as she could. His growls of pleasure shivered across her as he gathered up her dress and then reached behind her, lifting the fabric and tucking it into the back. Ass exposed, he slid his hands from her bottom to her back beneath her bra, then down again. With each shift of her hips, he groaned deliciously, and soon, she began moving a little bit faster.

His head rested against the headrest, and he watched her take him. Those bedroom eyes of his showed nothing but an affection that was as real as it was true. Gazing into those eyes, shields she didn't know were there started to crack, and feelings she didn't know were bandaged began to bleed.

Tears sprang to her eyes, and as one leaked out, he grabbed her waist with one hand, keeping her pressed tightly against him. The other came to her face and brushed the tear away. "Now what are those about?" he asked softly.

This wasn't her. She wasn't the emotional one. "It feels...."

"It feels *what?*"

"I don't know how we get this so right and yet..."

His eyes locked fiercely onto hers and softened. "We also get it so very wrong."

Another tear leaked from her eye, and he watched it travel down her cheek before he leaned up and a kissed it away. "Just be here, for as long as we can. That's what I want, Rae. I want you present. I want the side of you that isn't planning, who isn't thinking of what if's, who's just with me. Here. Now. Can you do that?"

"Yes," she whispered, somehow seeing so much of herself in Travis's eyes.

He fought emotion, she saw that across his expression, as he gripped her bottom, helping her rock back and forth. She placed her hands against the back of the seat and started shifting her hips, until neither of them was talking anymore. But she didn't have to hear the words coming from his mouth; she could see what he wanted to say in his eyes. All the barriers around the emotional lines she didn't want to cross came tumbling down around them as she pressed her lips against his. This wasn't heat, wasn't lust, it was so much more than that. *Desire…*

Love…

"Oh, God," she whispered, as he gripped one breast and nipped the taut bud.

Then she let it all go. She lost ten years' worth of cravings on his body, wildly riding him, bouncing up and down, sliding on his cock in perfect rhythm, taking him how she'd dreamed of taking him in her fantasies. She wasn't a young girl anymore, and she showed him without words how much she'd missed him. His constant, low groans encouraged her, and as he placed his head between her breasts, grunting with the force of her inner walls tightening around him, she slammed down on him harder.

The sweet pleasure was rising, and she bounced, hard and fast atop him. Sweat slid down her back as she gripped the seat behind them and worked herself over him more feverishly, her moans becoming faster, closer together. But then he grabbed her ass and took control, grinding her against him, and she moaned louder and louder, her hand now pressed against the back windshield.

"Travis," she screamed, breaking apart around him.

"Rae," he roared, bucking and jerking beneath her, somehow merging the past and present into one.

CHAPTER 7

Long before the movie finished, but done with being any-where except in a bed enjoying Rae outside the confines of the small space of the truck, Travis held the door open for her at the hotel on Main Street he'd been staying at since he arrived in Catfish Creek.

The historic hotel had a reputation for being haunted and was the oldest, continuously operating lodging establishment west of the Mississippi. It really came as no surprise that it hosted the guests from the reunion, as it was one of the hot spots in Catfish Creek.

As Rae passed by him and entered the building, she gave him a warm smile, and the flowery hints of her perfume teased his senses. He groaned, surprised how a scent could tempt him so much and began wondering if his bed at the hotel was a bet-ter idea for tonight than going back to her place after he picked up a few things.

He waited for a couple he remembered from math class to exit, then he let the doors shut behind him and joined Rae inside the three-story Victorian. Even now, he noted some other classmates in the oval lobby, some checking out at the registration desk surrounded by the Renaissance Corinthian columns, and others heading to the grand ballroom for a late dinner. It was amazing how many people had remained after the reunion. He guessed he wasn't the only one with unfinished business in Catfish Creek.

As he caught up with Rae, she glanced at him with that sweet smile and said, "You know, I was thinking, instead of just picking up some of your clothes, doesn't it make sense to cancel your reservation and come stay with me? I mean, it's kinda silly that you're paying for this room when you're not even staying here."

"If you want me to stay with you, I'm game," he said, smiling back at her, "but I don't need to worry about money, Rae."

"Right." She rolled her eyes. "I guess staying here won't break your bank."

No, it certainly wouldn't, but he knew he wasn't alone in becoming successful since high school. "I'm sure it wouldn't break yours either."

She barked a loud laugh. "Why do you say that?"

"You've done well for yourself, have you not?" he asked with an arched brow.

"It depends on your definition of 'well,'" she said, her hand brushing against his as they strode past the ballroom's entrance toward the elevators. "In terms of a vet clinic, I guess I've done okay. Compared to a rock star, I make pocket change."

He chuckled, reaching for her hand, and she stopped dead and stared at him with wide eyes. "What's wrong?" he asked.

She slowly glanced down to their linked hands and then looked back at him again, giving his hand a squeeze. "Is this okay?"

He frowned. "Why wouldn't it be okay?"

"We're in public."

"So?"

She looked around them before her concerned gaze met his again. "You're not worried someone will take a picture and sell the photograph to the media?"

Ah, now he saw what her anxiety was all about, but it was irrelevant. "Would I be upset if the media captured us together?" He slid his free hand across her back, bringing her nice and close against him. "Is that what you're asking?"

Cheeks flushed, she nodded.

"No, Rae, that's not something I'm worried about. I just hope if they do capture us, we give them something good to print." Her eyes grew wider in the seconds before he sealed his mouth over hers, and he hoped someone did catch them and that this would be all over the media tomorrow. It'd be the first time he felt as if the world got a real look into his life.

Rae kept up with his kiss, but when she stepped closer and cradled his body intimately, he broke the kiss, chuckling. "We might not want to give the media *that* kind of show."

She laughed with him. "True enough."

He released her and brought them back to the original conversation. "As I was saying, you must be doing well for yourself, considering you're thinking about opening another clinic."

She stopped again, and when he glanced over his shoulder, he found her brows furrowed, obviously confused. "How did you know I'm thinking about opening another clinic?" she asked.

He'd never been good at backpedaling, especially with her. Somehow, she always got the truth out of him. He parted his lips to stop his mouth from running away from him—because he wasn't sure he was ready to lay his truth bare for her—when a blistering voice said behind him, "Jesus Christ, Travis, there you are."

Travis glanced over his shoulder to find Scott, his manager, bursting into the hotel, icy blue eyes narrowed on him. Scott's cheeks were beet-red, and the vein in the center of his forehead was throbbing, looking a moment away from exploding. "Have you lost your fucking mind?" Scott howled, throwing up his hands.

His manager could intimidate. He was tall, brooding, and he didn't have a problem with the ladies. But Travis was a second away from laying his good friend out. "Come again?" he bit off.

"You can't turn off your goddamn phone," Scott practically sneered. "I've been calling and calling, and now"—he glanced around the hotel's lobby like he'd entered a sewer—"I'm here in this place, and I've been waiting for you all fucking day."

The anger coming from Scott was palpable; the man was not to be trifled with. That was one of the reasons Travis respected him. Scott got shit done. Not appreciating that side of Scott now, however, Travis heaved a long sigh and glanced at Rae next to him. Her arms were crossed, eyes on Scott. "I'm sorry. This is, Scott, my manager," he told her, uncrossing her arms and taking her hand. "Apparently, he's lost all his manners. Do you mind if I have a minute?"

"Oh…your manager." She gave Scott another quick look before she looked at Travis again and gave a tight smile. "Of course, no worries. I'll just be outside."

But that smile wasn't the real and warm expression he loved. This one hinted at sadness, and the darkness reached her eyes, Goddamn it, he felt it, too. Things had changed between them at the drive-in. Before, when he'd touched her, she felt like the old Rae. But tonight, she'd felt like a woman with life experience. She felt as if she wanted to fight for something they'd never experienced before. Like she wanted to fight for the future, not stay in the past.

With emotion beginning to claw at his chest, he watched her turn and walk away, and with every step she took, he got colder and colder. He waited until she was outside before he turned back to Scott. "If you ever talk to me like that again, or make Rae feel uncomfortable, this partnership is done."

Scott folded his arms, standing firm and strong. "For fuck's sake, Travis, you pay me to ensure your life is managed. If I let you run away from your obligations, then what kind of manager would I be? Tell me that."

He waited for the people that were staring at them to walk by, clearly hearing Scott's rage before he asked, "What obligations?"

"The show tomorrow for the charity for the children's hospital," Scott snapped, shoving his hands into his pockets. His cheeks flamed red, and his voice was low with controlled fury. "The one that *I* promised you would be at." The vein still protruded from the middle of his forehead, looking even bigger now. "The one where if you don't show up, I will be responsible for letting down a charity that supports sick and dying children."

Dread began to spill into Travis. Fuck, how could he have forgotten? Again and again, he wasn't himself. He'd thought coming back to the reunion would set his mind straight. He thought it was working. "Shit, fuck, I'm sorry." He ran a hand through his hair, feeling the culpability drown him.

"It's fine that you forgot," Scott added, softer now. "It's why you have me. Your schedule is full, and you need someone to help you manage it all." He gave Travis a measured look before glancing at his watch. "But you cannot shut me out like that. You do that again, and I walk, Travis."

Travis nodded in agreement. "It won't happen again." Because he knew this was his only shot. He'd come back to Catfish

Creek in hopes that something would change…and he wasn't sure he'd had enough time to make that happen.

Scott took his phone from his pocket and glanced at the screen, a frown marring his face. "We have two hours before the next flight to New York." The redness in his cheeks began to lessen, and his voice lost its tight edge. "Which means, we've got time to get up to the room here and do a couple of interviews promoting the event."

"All right," Travis said, looking at the scuffed ceramic floor beneath his shoes.

Scott's long and heavy sigh filled the space around Travis before he said, "I take it all this was about that chick."

Travis nodded, words failing him.

"Why don't you bring her with you?" Scott offered, his voice back to its usual tone, even sympathy showed in his eyes. "Or, if you want to come back here after the show, your schedule is clear for the next couple days."

Again, Travis nodded; dread further filling him at the fact that he controlled nothing. A weight settled on his chest, and he felt the happiness he'd experienced the past couple of days crumble around him. Just as he'd felt time and time again, he was a *thing*, a pawn used to suit everyone else. His happiness wasn't real. It was something written on a calendar. How fucking depressing was that?

"All right, this is good. We can make this happen," Scott said as his phone began to ring. "While you deal with her, I'll pack up your stuff." He held out his hand, and with the other, pressed his phone to his ear. "Price here. Yes. Yes. We'll be ready for that interview soon. No, not that reporter, she's an uptight bitch. Get the other one. Yeah, that one."

Numb and cold, Travis grabbed his wallet and took out his key card, then handed it to Scott, who spun on his heels and headed to the elevator, saying nothing more to Travis.

Standing in the lobby, watching the world whiz by as it seemed to do now, Travis had all the answers to his questions. He'd come to the reunion to see if what he'd had with Rae was real. If he'd truly been happier then or if he'd created it all in his mind. But he knew, standing there, watching his life pass, this thing with Rae was more than happiness, it was his home.

She's home.

If only she felt the same way about him.

—🙠—

A hard lump had formed in Rae's throat the second before she turned away from Travis. Even once she made it outside, and after she'd sat on the bench, staring out at the quiet street, the lump only thickened. Everything suddenly felt very wrong.

Main Street was quiet with only a few pedestrians walking down the road, and a couple of cars going by, and even though the night couldn't have been prettier with its clear sky and spar-kling stars above her, the world seemed to fly by. She'd known this was coming—of course, she did—but now that Travis was leaving, she felt totally and completely unprepared.

Before the reunion, life had been simple and uncomplicated. Sure, maybe she'd been a little restless trying to find that spark that once drove her. But these past days, she'd been reminded that something important was missing from her life, and she couldn't help but think now that that *something* had everything to do with Travis.

His kiss, his touch, his company—she'd forgotten the magnificence of being loved. Hell, thinking about it now, she wondered if she'd forced herself to forget so she could get over him. Because these past days, especially after tonight, perfect warmth had filled her, making the world seem a bit fuller and brighter. But now, a cloud seemed to hang overhead, the cold darkness threatening to overtake her.

"Rae."

She glanced sideways, finding Travis only a foot away. The softness in his eyes stole her breath. She'd seen those eyes before. It's how he looked when he said goodbye. There were a hundred things to say, but, "We're right back where we were ten years ago, huh?" was what eventually came out.

Travis nodded and then took a seat next to her, hanging his head and resting his arms on his legs. "But it's different. We're different."

"How are we so different?" she asked, wrapping her arms around herself, fighting off the chill.

"We're older. Wiser." He turned his head, revealing emotion-packed eyes. "More settled, maybe. Less driven…I don't know."

She gave him a soft smile in agreement. They'd both changed and gained life experience, that couldn't be questioned. They'd both chased down their dreams and caught them. Yet, right now, it seemed as if that was the wrong thing to do. At least, her heart saw it that way. "It's funny, isn't it?"

He glanced sideways at her. "What's funny?"

"Life," she explained with a little shrug. "How so much time can pass, and yet, sometimes, it feels like none has passed at all." She paused, trying to collect her thoughts. "I can't help but wonder why this is happening to us again." His brows furrowed, eyes intent on hers, but he stayed silent as she added, "You know that I'm not a huge believer in fate."

"You believe you create your own destiny."

She gave a soft smile. "Exactly. That's what I've always believed."

"But you don't believe that now?"

She heaved a long sigh and glanced out at the road as a car went by. "I just don't know anymore. It's like, why are you here…" His lips parted, and she waved him off. "I know. I know. For the reunion. But it just seems too perfect." She saw his eyes warm when she said, "Too planned, almost."

"Like maybe fate had a hand in bringing us back together?"

She smiled. "Maybe, but my logical brain has a hard time believing that."

ROCK STAR

His soft chuckle slid across her as she looked out at the road again and watched the bustle of the city she knew and loved. Everything had made sense ten years ago. When she'd said goodbye to Travis, she reconciled his leaving in her mind. He needed to go to make something of himself, and she needed to stay to do the same.

"I don't want you to go," she said, finally looking at him.

His eyes were locked onto hers. "I can come back," he said gently. "I'll come back if you want me to."

How easy would it be for her to open her mouth and say, *yes, please come back,* but then how fair would that be? His band was in New York. She couldn't do a long-distance relationship. She needed her man with her, all the time, not only a handful of days out of the month.

She'd known the complications of this going into the weekend. She'd made a deal with herself. This weekend…*just sex,* then he would go. "We both know that making a promise to each other to make this work would complicate everything, and we also know that we won't do complicated."

"It *would* complicate things," he eventually said, running a hand through his hair. "It's not the life either of us wants."

"We don't do drama. We don't do difficult."

He chuckled. "We like life easy."

It was something they'd always said to each other. She searched his eyes, and it didn't take long for her to see what he was thinking—and feeling. Regret. "You don't have to feel bad, you know."

His brows furrowed, and she hastily glanced away from all the emotion in his eyes, unable to stand it. "We both knew what this was," she added. "We also knew you'd eventually leave."

He tucked his finger under her chin, garnering her attention. "Yeah, we did, but it's still shit, Rae. I wasn't expecting to leave tonight. I thought we'd have more time." He paused, dragged his fingers across her jawline, igniting that burn within that he drew out so easily. "I have a show that I forgot about, and it's for a children's charity."

"You don't need to explain, Travis," she said, telling herself she needed to be okay with this. His life was in New York. Hers was in Catfish Creek. Her friends lived here, and her family, too. Her life was here. That wouldn't change.

"Actually, I think I do need to explain." He hesitated, and she noted the strain between his brows when he continued. "The music...that's all I am, Rae. Without it, I'm nothing."

"I know," she reminded him, taking up his hand and holding it in both of hers. "Again, you don't need to explain. I understand."

"I *do* need to explain," he said again, voice thick. "Because, this...you..." He pulled his hand back and cupped her face. "Believe me, it's everything, too. It always has been. You're the only one that I want, Rae. I never said it enough before, and I hope you truly hear me now. All I want is you."

She gave him the smile she knew he needed to see and placed her hands around his, fighting against the sudden tears welling in her eyes. "I know that, too. I've always known that." And she did, truly. Because him loving her had never been a question in her mind. Or even her loving him. Life seemed to get in the way. "But it won't change the fact that your life isn't here with me and it won't ever be. You outgrew Catfish a long time ago."

"I'm not always on the road," he told her, and she saw the pleading in his eyes. "Sometimes, yes. But other times, I'm at home in New York."

"I know," she whispered.

He stared at her hard, as if he wanted her to fix all this. "Then what do we do?"

She shut her eyes, willing strength. "There's nothing we can do," she admitted, unable to deal with the problems they faced. "We can't change the obstacles in our way. They're there, plain as day. And maybe this was all we got, one more moment in time to remember how lucky we were to have had each other."

She saw him flinch and swore she could see the coldness rip through him. He dropped his hands from her face, lowering them back onto his knees, and stared out at the street, silently lost in his thoughts. The minutes passed, the quiet becoming more and more awkward as the seconds drew on.

"Besides," she added, attempting to ease the tension. "It's easier this time, don't you think?"

His eyes narrowed on her. "You think leaving you… *again…*is easy for me?"

"A little," she said with a slight shrug. "We knew we had this weekend, a little taste of what we had before, and that's what we got. I don't regret it, do you?"

"Do I regret you being in my arms again?" He snorted, then had his hands around her face again, staring at her intently, stripping her bare. "No, Rae, that I could never regret. But I do regret that somehow, no matter how much time passes between us, we can't seem to get this right."

"Or maybe we do get it right," she offered. "Maybe this is all we can be, all that we're meant to be."

"Still so fucking practical," he growled, brushing his thumb across her cheek. "Is that your final conclusion?"

She nodded. "It's what makes sense, and as you well know, I do like logic."

He paused and then slowly shook his head. "Why does this make sense to you?"

"Because if something doesn't ever seem to work out, it's because it's not meant to."

She regretted the words the moment they left her mouth because of the way he cringed, clearly hurt by them.

He didn't back away, though, and it'd be so easy to get lost in the way he watched her. The way he loved her. "So, that's it?" he asked softly. "I love you like this, and yet I still leave you."

She stopped herself from flinching. This was punishing them both, and she didn't want him to hurt, that was the last thing she wanted. She leaned forward and kissed his mouth gently, then added, "That's reality. That's life. That's what we knew would happen after this weekend ended." When she leaned away, she stared into his eyes, showing him she was okay. "You'll keep in touch?"

"I can't stay away," he said, never taking his eyes off hers.

Before she lost her nerve and allowed herself to feel what she knew he was feeling, she rose, emotion squeezing her throat. "Bye, Travis."

He rose then, standing in front of her. She fought the emotion as he stared at her hard, then it threatened to escape her as he wrapped his arms around her, hugging her in the way only he could. Strong. Warm. Like home. "Goodbye, Rae."

Then she did what she knew he couldn't do.

With tears in her eyes, she walked away.

CHAPTER 8

Minutes later, the place that had always been home to Rae didn't even look the same anymore as she passed store after store on Main Street. It was like the world had been turned upside down, redesigned, and then reassembled again after this weekend with Travis.

Despite the hot and dry air, a chill ran through her when she strode beneath the street light, passing over the lines in the cement sidewalk. Before the reunion, she had felt restless. Now, she felt utterly and hopelessly lost.

The rules had been clear. Hell, she'd set them. They got each other for a little while, and then he'd go home. Life would go on as it had for the last ten years. Though, she hadn't taken into account how much these past days with him would change her. It kind of snuck up on her.

She wasn't the same woman who'd walked through the reunion doors; she knew that for a fact. Something had changed.

ROCK STAR

Something drastic in those tender spaces of her soul. No matter what she did, or how long she walked, she couldn't quite get her mind to settle back into that comfortable peace she'd become accustomed to.

The sidewalk came to an end, forcing her to look up. She waited for the light to turn green before she continued, walking toward her home instead of catching a cab. Air and exercise had to clear her head, right?

Lights glowed up ahead on the right side of the street, and in just a few steps, she passed the Hamburger Shack. In the corner of the restaurant, she spotted the booth that she and Travis used to sit in, now occupied by another teenage couple. With a small step forward, the past enveloped her.

Meat stacked upon meat stacked upon meat. Rae held back her chuckle, watching Travis bite into his giant-sized burger. "You know," she said from her side of the booth, "people have died from choking. It's a real threat that you should be worried about."

He swallowed his bite. "I sincerely doubt I'm going to die eating..."

"Inhaling," she corrected.

"Fine, inhaling a cheeseburger." He winked, took an even bigger bite, and said with a full mouth, "Besides, it's a damn good way to go."

She laughed loudly, and it felt good. The past days had been stressful and tense, and this break, doing something that they used to do all the time, was exactly what they needed. She glanced down, staring at her chicken wings, feeling her throat growing tighter and tighter. The clock was ticking, and the weakness inside her was growing bigger than her strength.

When she looked at him again, she found Travis focused on his burger. She couldn't stop the hurt from sounding in her voice. "Three days to go, huh?"

He glanced up through his lashes and studied her, and then darkness filled his warm eyes. He placed his burger down and wiped his hands on his napkin, then took one of hers in both of his. "Don't go there yet. Let's not think about it until we have to."

How could she not think about it? He was leaving her, and there was nothing she could to do stop him. Sure, she wanted him to chase his dreams. She just didn't want him moving to New York City to do it. She wanted him here. With her. Forever.

"Rae," he said firmly in response to what obviously showed in her expression. "Not yet, okay."

That's when she saw what he kept hidden very well. He was struggling to hang on, too. She forced a smile, knowing he needed that from her. "Okay, not yet. Promise."

Reality hit her as a body slammed into her side. "Sorry," she gasped. "I'm sorry."

"Watch where you're going," the man sneered.

Ice-cold now, she wrapped her arms around herself and kept walking toward home. Each step forward felt like she was going somewhere, but not moving at all. The world was all but still around her. This pain cutting through her was all too familiar, and as she passed the dress store, the last time she'd felt like this became vividly real again.

Rae stepped into the navy-blue lace dress that she didn't want. Hell, she hadn't even wanted to leave the house, but Mom had forced her. She pulled the straps onto her arms and then opened the curtain. Mom's bright smile should've warmed her, but it did nothing to stop the coldness that seemed to enter her the day Travis left—a feeling that had only gotten worse as the weeks went on.

"It won't always hurt like this, honey," Mom said, obviously sensing what was on Rae's mind. She entered the changing room, and in the mirror behind Rae, her gentle, green eyes warmed. "I promise. Each day, it will get better."

"But it's been a month now," Rae said, tears welling and spilling out. Dammit, this was why she didn't like to go out. She'd break into tears when she least expected it.

Mom settled the dress perfectly into place on Rae's shoulders. "The heart doesn't care how long it's been. It just takes time, my darling." She grabbed the zipper and began pulling it up. "I think this is the one."

Rae looked as the dress tightened around her, forming to her body and giving her good shape. But when she glanced up, all she saw were her eyes. Eyes that she didn't even recognize anymore. She'd always been happy, confident, and content.

This past month, all she felt was shattered and broken.

"See how pretty you look," Mom said, dragging her hands down Rae's arms. "It's a perfect dress for the cruise."

Rae smiled, giving her what she knew her mom needed. But she stopped listening to all the things her mom said, unable to feel, oddly numb to it all, until she said, "Trust me, my darling, one day you'll look back on this and realize Travis was a young love that truly mattered at the time, but a young love was all he was."

Standing on the street, staring at one of the dresses in the window, she knew her mom had been dead wrong. She never looked back and thought of Travis as a young love. He was her *one and only*. Her heart began to race, her palms growing sweaty as she glanced from left to right, realizing Travis was everywhere even though, soon, he'd be back in New York. Every square inch of Catfish Creek had a memory with Travis in it. And that's what had been the hardest part about moving on. He was etched into her soul, and without him here, the town felt…darker…lonelier…empty.

Instead of taking the long way, she turned left and entered the park. Maybe all she needed was to have a good, long cry, then she could center herself again. She strode beneath the lights guiding her way along the tree-lined path, finding the park busy as usual. The walkway was full of people, some on bikes, some taking a stroll, hand in hand with their loves. She felt like she was floating, heading somewhere but going nowhere, taking steps forward and yet somehow moving backward.

Up ahead, she spotted a tree, and her pace picked up naturally. There was a tingle in the back of her brain, a memory just on the surface, and when she reached the tree, tilting her head up to stare at the branches from underneath, she knew why.

The tree branches danced in the light wind, the moonlight casting a stunning glow over the park. She glanced back to Travis in front of her, and he smiled. "What are you up to?" she asked.

"Wooing you, as always," he said, twirling her out and then pulling her in close.

With people walking by, and him not caring, as usual, he placed a hand low on her body, holding her close as he began to dance with her.

"You truly don't care what people think of you, do you?" she asked, staring into the warmth of his eyes.

He leaned down close, bringing his mouth near hers. "I care what you think of me."

"Well, you know I love you, so that doesn't count."

He chuckled and pressed a little tighter on her back. "Come here, baby. Be close."

Somehow, he always made an awkward situation be okay. And right now, the world around her didn't matter. Only Travis did. She placed her head against his chest, shutting her eyes, losing herself in him.

Round and round they went in a circle, right there under the stars, as he sang her favorite song softly in her ear. She knew some girls wanted the quarterback or the coolest guy in school, but after meeting Travis in chemistry class, she'd only had eyes for him. And she was only too happy that he saw her, too. She'd always heard that love took work, but loving him was all too easy.

Maybe that was him. His passion. His truth.

He knew how to love someone.

When he sang the last note, she looked up, and he smiled down at her. Did everyone feel this way? So madly in love, their heart might burst wide open.

They stopped dancing, and his hands slid up her arms to cup her face. "I wanna kiss you under the moonlight," he said, bowing his head, bringing his mouth close to hers. "And love you 'til the sun comes up."

"Always the romantic." She smiled. "Forever the songwriter."

"I can't help it." He brushed his nose against hers, weakening her knees. "You inspire me."

She grinned, maybe stupidly by some standards, but she didn't care. Her heart was so full, so warm. "I love you."

He grinned and dipped her back, and just before he kissed her, he said, "I love you, too, baby."

"Miss."

Rae startled and gasped, trying to force herself back into the present, but she felt as if she were tumbling. She sucked in a harsh breath as her throat tightened, and she clawed at her chest, trying to get air. She remembered the pain when he left, but there had been such happiness, so much love. Yes, he was passionate, but he loved her more than she ever thought she deserved to be loved.

How had she forgotten what it felt like to be loved by him? He'd been here. She let him leave…*again.*

Shadows seemed to form around her, coldness seeping in to steal all the warmth from her soul. Her legs wobbled, and the world began to summersault around her when a sudden hand grasped her shoulder.

"Daniel, help her."

Rae whirled around, facing the concerned voice behind her. She found an elderly couple staring wide-eyed at her.

"Miss," the man with the kind eyes said again, reaching for her arms. "Are you all right?"

"No, I'm not." She fought to get air into her lungs, feeling the ground drop out from beneath her. "No, I'm not okay at all. I can't breathe. Please, help me."

CHAPTER 9

Two hours later, Rae sat on the hospital bed, legs dangling over the side. She stared out at her empty room with its plain yellow walls and sterile stench, wondering how in the hell she got there. *This* wasn't her. She never fell apart, certainly not enough to warrant a hospital visit and a Xanax. Whatever happened between the time Travis returned to now, left her feeling like she was barely hanging on. She'd known dipping back into the past would be dangerous. She knew there would be consequences. But now she realized how steep they'd be.

Without Travis in Catfish Creek anymore, everything seemed entirely wrong.

A sudden knock on the door snapped her head up, and then instant relief and warmth stole all the coldness inside as she found two brunettes standing in the doorway. Her best friends always made everything better. The shortest of the three friends, Kate, smiled gently, while Tessa twirled her straight hair around her finger, clearly on edge.

Rae wasn't. She wanted the hell out of there. Pronto! "Oh, my God," she gasped, waving them in, "get me the hell out of here." Apparently, telling the doctors that she was fine and could take a taxi home wasn't good enough. But, luckily, Kate and Tessa had been home and able to fetch her, promising to be her babysitters for the evening.

Kate reached the bedside first, but Tessa was the one who asked, "I'm glad to see that you're still you. The nurse said she'd be in soon to discharge you, but for now, you need to explain to us why you're here."

God, she didn't want to admit this. At all. But the truth was a promise between them. Always had been. Always would be. "Well, apparently, I had a panic attack."

The way they froze statue-still was almost laughable…*almost*.

Kate blinked a couple of times, but her light green eyes remained wide. "*You* had a panic attack?"

Rae nodded and gave a tight smile. "I know, it's shocking. I wouldn't have believed it was possible either. But it happened, and I scared the living shit out of two elderly people. Poor couple, I think they thought I was dying. The woman thought I was choking. The man kept smacking my back."

Tessa giggled, hand on her mouth. "That's not funny, but is still kinda funny."

"It's okay to laugh," Rae agreed with a smile, which felt good in all this confusion. "The whole thing is totally unbelievable. I didn't even think I could be emotional enough for a panic attack."

"It's never happened before?" Kate asked.

"Never." Rae paused, studying Kate. There was a twinkle in her best friend's eyes that hadn't been there the last time she'd seen her, which was at the reunion. But, of course, that felt like a lifetime ago with everything that had happened. "Okay, enough about me for a minute. What's up with you?"

"Well," Kate drawled, eyes squinting. "I wasn't going to say anything right now, considering you're here in the hospital, but I'm guessing that's out of the question since you have that answer-me look on your face."

"Totally out of the question," Rae said. "I spent an hour talking to a therapist about myself when I didn't want to talk about me at all." She waved Kate on. "I want to know what's behind that look."

Kate laughed quietly and took a seat in the chair next to the bed. She crossed her legs, displaying the butterfly tattoo on her ankle. "Keeping it simple because I think you've been through enough tonight, I've picked Denver to go to college."

"Denver," Rae said, surprised. Weeks ago, Kate had been undecided between Wyoming and Denver, but that was also because she had her two kids to think about, too. Life was a lot more complicated for Kate than it'd been for either Tessa or Rae. "Okay, this I have to hear. What swayed your decision toward Denver?"

Kate played with her dark brown hair and grinned. "Grayson Cleary, and the fact that I'm in love with him."

"Wait. *What?*" Rae pressed her hands flat against the bed, staring hard at a laughing Kate and Tessa before she managed, "Are you serious?"

"Totally serious," Kate said, softness reaching her eyes. "Seems like fate is actually being kind for once."

Rae's heart nearly exploded, and she was off the bed and on her feet a second later, all but lunging at Kate. She wrapped her arms around her tightly. "I'm so, so, so happy for you, and for the kids. I didn't know it was that serious between you and Grayson." Hell, all she knew was that things between Kate and Grayson were hot, but she didn't realize they'd become so heavy.

"Oh, honey, it wasn't serious"—Kate leaned away and shrugged, still smiling from ear-to-ear—"until it was, and then there was no going back. The kids are happy. I'm happy."

"Y'all deserve this happiness," Rae said, glancing into her friend's eyes, seeing the joy, unable to stop from getting misty-eyed. Kate hadn't had it easy, not with her jackass of an ex-husband, Jason, and for once, the good guys came out on top, and thank God for that.

Feeling like the world was maybe a little brighter now than it'd been earlier, Rae looked at Tessa, who stood at the door, a special little twinkle in her eye, as well. "You're unusually quiet over there," Rae pointed out, moving back to the bed. "Why? Do you have news, too?"

"We weren't supposed to talk about this tonight," Tessa said with a frown, crossing her arms over her chest.

"Tessa," Rae said seriously, pulling up her legs to sit cross-legged. "I'm sitting in a hospital because I had a panic attack. I think I'm due for some good news, so spill."

Tessa paused a few seconds longer then sighed. "Okay, well, do you remember when…" She hesitated again and then laughed softly. "How about I keep it simple like Kate did? If I told you everything I've been through lately, I doubt you'd even believe me anyway. So, here goes. Things were batshit crazy, but everything's good now, perfect, really. Remember Derek Spencer?"

Rae thought back, recalling that Derek used to hang around with their crowd back in the day, though Rae didn't know much more about him than that. "Yeah, I think so. Tall, with black hair. Went into the military, right?"

"Yeah, that's him," Tessa said, her blue eyes gleaming. "So, we're together now. He's got a year left in the marines, and I've decided to wait for him."

"I'm still not sure I'd be okay with such a long wait," Kate said gently, obviously not judging but concerned.

"He's worth the wait, believe me," Tessa said with a soft smile, the same gleam back in her blue eyes. "But I don't plan on waiting all by myself either, so, here's where you come in," she said to Rae. "Got a dog for me?"

"You want to adopt a dog?" Rae asked, feeling a bit winded by all these rapid changes.

Tessa shrugged. "Is that okay?"

"Of course, that's okay," Rae said. "In fact, it's more than okay. It's about time you got some fluffy love, and we've got a couple of real cuties back at the clinic right now available for adoption. Go on over tomorrow and take a look."

"Great." Tessa smiled, more honestly than Rae had seen in a long time.

Rae needed this, she decided. The chill, the stress, the pain was easing by the minute with her friends there. She turned to Kate again and asked, "Do you want to go back to your place tonight so I can start helping you pack?" The moment the words left her mouth, emotion clawed at her throat.

Kate exchanged a long look with Tessa. "Ah, listen, Rae, I know you love me and all, but I'll come back to see you, and you can come see me, too."

"No, it's not that." Tears she couldn't control began to well in her eyes, and her hands started to shake. "Dammit, it's happening again. What is this? What's wrong with me?"

Kate reached up from where she sat, placing a hand on Rae's knee. "Taking a guess here, but did something happen with Travis?"

Rae wiped the tears off her face again and looked at Tessa, who shrugged. "I caught Kate up on all the happenings in your life."

"And I was happy to hear the news, too," Kate said, voice gentle. "It's about time you dusted off the cobwebs and actually acted like you're twenty-eight, not eighty-nine."

Kate meant it as a joke. Rae should've laughed. But Rae's chin quivered, and before she could drop her head into her hands and sob, her best friends were there, hands pressing comfortingly against her.

"Honey, I'm sorry," Kate said gently.

"What's got you so torn up?" Tessa asked, rubbing Rae's back. "Talking about it always helps."

She reined in her cries, forcing herself to hold it together. "He's gone."

"What do you mean...*gone*?" Kate asked.

Rae dropped her hands, grabbed a tissue off the side table next to her, and dabbed her eyes. "Travis is likely on his way back to New York as we speak."

Kate's fingers tightened on Rae's leg, and she shook her head, obviously confused. "Wait. Why?"

"Why wouldn't he?" Rae countered, glancing down to the tissue in her hands. "His life isn't here, it's in New York. I mean... this shouldn't have happened anyway. It all still feels like some big dream." She glanced from Kate to Tessa, watching a couple of nurses walk past the doorway before addressing them again. "And why in the hell do you both look so surprised?"

"I guess..." Tessa said, then gave a half shrug. "I guess I just expected you two to run off and elope or something."

Kate gave a firm nod, slowly dropping back into her seat, but keeping her hand on Rae's leg. "That was the endgame here. When Tessa and I talked, we were both sure that this was like your guys' second chance at love. One you'd both take."

"I mean, really, Rae," Tessa said softly, "you two belong together. We've all known that since high school."

Rae wished she knew that because, right now, she didn't know anything. Everything was changing. Kate, her sidekick, was moving away. Tessa's life was settled and on a focused path. As for Rae's life? *What a mess!* "Belonging together has never been our problem. It's staying in the same state that we can't seem to get right."

Kate nibbled her lip, watching Rae closely. "But if that makes sense to you logically, then why are you so rattled and… well, to be put it bluntly, losing it?"

"Because, apparently, him leaving me this time was a million times worse than before. It's like my logical mind just shut down, and my broken heart bled out," Rae said, dabbing away the rest of her tears that lingered on her face. "Hence, the panic attack. It happened after he left."

Tessa studied Rae intently. Finally, she got her I've-got-everything-figured-out look and stated, "I know it might sound weird and all, but your panic attack is kinda long overdue, don't you think?"

"No, actually I don't," Rae retorted. "It was horrible, and I hope to never feel anything like that ever again."

"Just listen to me for a sec," Tessa gently pressed, leaning a hip against the edge of the bed and folding her arms. "For as long as we've all been friends, you've always been the strong one, the logical one, the responsible and sensible one."

"She's got you pegged," Kate agreed.

Tessa gave a firm nod and continued. "You lead with your head, which of course is why we love you. You're the stable one, the dependable one. You always give the best advice and help keep us on track, but maybe you don't do that enough with yourself."

Rae glanced down at the tissue in her hands, her throat tightening again like it had on the street, like she couldn't get enough air. In the presence of her two best friends, the women who knew her better than anyone, she let her strength falter. When she looked at them again, real and raw tears in her eyes, she did nothing to shield her pain. "I'm not that strong person right now."

Tessa took Rae's hand and squeezed it. "I see that."

Kate squeezed her other hand. "But *why* aren't you that person right now? That's what you've got to ask yourself. What happened between you two that's left you like this?"

"Everything happened," Rae explained. "It's like this past weekend, I got a taste of what it felt like to be loved by him again, but it was different, it was better." Her voice blistered. "I feel broken without him."

"More broken than you felt the last time he left?"

She nodded. "I feel like I can't bandage up all the shattered pieces."

"Have you told him that?" Tessa asked.

"No," Rae admitted.

"Maybe you should," Kate said simply. "To be honest, Rae, I think you're missing something very important here."

Tessa clearly knew what she meant. Her eyes lit up, and she added, "It's why it's so surprising he left."

Rae felt like the ground was swallowing her up. She wasn't following anything. And how strange was that? "What am I missing?" she asked.

Kate offered, "Why would a guy who had it all come back to his high school reunion?"

"Yes," Tessa said. "And why would a guy be so wrapped up in a girl for a weekend and then just leave?"

Rae had all the reasons Travis told her, but something stopped her. For some reason, she couldn't open her mouth and give the reasons he'd given. They no longer made sense. She kept asking herself why he came back. She kept thinking there had to be a bigger reason. Sure, he'd explained himself to her, but now—maybe because of the awareness and truth in her friends' eyes—she most definitely believed he wasn't telling her everything.

"You were planning on opening another clinic…"

How had he known that about her?

She stopped pondering the things he'd told her, and she grasped what her friends must have realized, too. He seemed to know things about her, like her thinking about opening another clinic. Things he simply didn't have to know. But there was something else…something that made her realize she hadn't seen things clearly.

For a guy who seemed unsure about his life, he seemed very much decided about her the entire time. "You know what," she said, seeing the world through new eyes, watching her friends nod at her, clearly reading where her thoughts were taking her. "Maybe, through all this, through all the things I wanted to know about him, I have been asking the wrong question all along."

CHAPTER 10

I wanna kiss you under the moonlight.
And love you 'til the sun comes up.

The final lyric rippled across Travis as it left his mouth and burned into his soul, as it had the night he'd written the song about Rae. A night that had been one of his worst, where he felt each second that he missed her. After that night, he'd forced himself to forget her, only to survive. His fingers slowly lowered from his guitar, his head bowed, the warmth in his soul gone. He'd been told about men who died empty, and right now, he believed he would be among them.

His chance to claim the woman who filled him up had faded into the shadows as it had ten years ago. Only this time, he hurt more. Dammit, he bled more. Sure, logic told him to stay away, as it had before. But his heart didn't want to hear it this time. He was having a harder time accepting that their time had come and gone and that they simply would never be an *us*. Just as the crippling darkness sank her claws into him, a roar of thunderous applause broke him out of his cold longing.

Numb and aching, he lifted his head, suddenly reminded that he wasn't alone. No, he was back in New York City, miles away from Rae. Defeated and depleted, he stared out into the crowd of nameless faces. They were on their feet, screaming their praise. None of them knew the true him. None of them knew the meaning behind that song, or how damn hard it was for him to sing it tonight. None of them saw his pain and the wounds in his heart. Years back when he'd written that song for Rae, he had hoped that once she heard it, she'd come to him. That she'd remember that night when they danced in the park and how special it had been.

She never came then.

Nor did she come now.

And even at the reunion, she didn't mention anything about the song when she'd heard him sing it there.

"Travis, man, are you all right?"

He turned his head, finding his bass player and backup vocalist, Zander, staring at him with concerned, soft brown eyes. Tall and lanky, Zander and Travis had been friends since Travis moved to New York City after his agent had introduced them. Travis couldn't lie and nod like he usually did. He didn't know what he was feeling; he only knew that the days he'd been back in New York had seemed like his darkest days yet.

ROCK STAR

Aware that everyone was waiting on him now, he inhaled deeply and slid off the stool, stepping away from his mic. With the crowd still going wild around him, he glanced over his shoulder at the rest of the guys in the band behind him, his longtime friends. It felt right being here with them, sharing this dream, but without Rae here, too, only half of him felt settled. Perhaps because of all the years he'd endured the tortuous hell of not having her because he knew she was making her dreams come true. But now, he knew she'd nearly fulfilled those dreams, and without her here, he felt as if everything he had, all that he was crumbled around him.

But he couldn't fall…not yet. "Let's finish this," he said to Zander, who regarded him now with blatant concern, reinforcing how bad Travis actually looked.

He couldn't fake it anymore. He wasn't okay.

Determined to finish the show and get home, he glanced at the crowd again, and something drew his gaze to the right of the stage. He squinted his eyes, as nothing should have been there. When he finally caught sight of who stood there, he froze. Sure he couldn't be seeing things right, he blinked, again and again, but the figure remained.

Rae.

With shaky hands, he unhooked his guitar from the speaker and slid the strap over his head and the instrument across his back. Not caring about anything but the beauty watching him, he crossed the stage to her.

"Travis," Zander yelled out to him.

There would be no stopping him. Part of him wondered if, in his pain, he imagined her standing there. But the closer he got, the more he saw her eyes widen in surprise. That's how he knew he wasn't dreaming. Because if he were, she'd be in his arms kissing him by now.

When he reached her, she cracked a smile, and said, "Um, you weren't supposed to come off the stage like that. Shouldn't you go back out there?"

He stood so close to her, yet was still so far away, his muscles quivering. "Why are you here?" He had to know.

She paused, and it was then that he noticed that his drummer had begun putting on a show for the crowd. He couldn't care about anything going on around him, but focused solely on her mouth when she finally said, "Before I answer that, I want you to know that I know what you did for me."

"What did I do?" he asked softly.

"You loved me." She took one step forward. "You left days ago because you loved me like I once loved you." Tears welled in her eyes, and that's when he grabbed her, holding onto her arms. "And you loved me enough to never ask me to leave my friends and family to be with you," she finished.

He held her tightly, never wanting to let go. "How could I take you away from all the things *you* love?"

A tear slid down her cheek, and he watched it move slowly down her face as she added, "I'm here because I realized I asked you the wrong question all along. And that's not something I can live with. Not anymore."

"What question?" he wondered aloud.

She took one more step, nearly pressing against him now. "Why didn't you tell me you wanted me to move to New York with you?"

Seemed simple enough, but it was anything but simple. "Because I know what it means to have a dream and see it through. What that dream can give to a person…the happiness it brings." He waved back out to the stage, where his band was keeping the crowd entertained. "How could I ask anyone to walk away from their life and give up everything for me, all because I need them desperately? I couldn't live with myself if I did that to you."

"You needed to give me the opportunity to decide for myself," she retorted. "You never asked me, just like I never really asked you ten years ago if you wanted to go to New York. I just pushed you to chase your dreams and ran after mine. We have to stop doing that to each other."

He cupped her face, sliding his hands across her damp cheeks. "It was right at the time. We needed to go after our dreams, but you're right, we should have talked about it."

"Yeah, then and now," she said. "It seems like in our efforts to keep things easy, we forgot that we can do hard things if we talk about them and figure out how to do them together." Some heady emotion crossed her face as she added, "And I think it's time for us to make that happen." She stepped out of his arms and went behind a wall, returning a second later with a cat carrier in her hands. "I really hope you and Harry can get along because we're moving in."

When his mind finally accepted the truth that this was happening, he rushed to Rae, grabbed her, and awkwardly hugged her with the damn cat carrier between them and his guitar on his back. He cursed, gently taking Harry from her and placing him down on the floor as the cat meowed, clearly protesting his imprisonment. Travis cupped Rae's face again, emotion clawing at his chest. "Jesus, Rae, tell me you're serious."

"Yes, I'm serious." She laughed. "I brought my cat, and we're moving in, so I'm not sure how that can get any more serious."

He sealed his mouth over hers, his emotion burning in his kiss. "Tell me you're not leaving."

"I'm not leaving."

He stared at her deeply and promised, "I'll do everything I can to help you set up your next clinic here. And we'll buy the perfect home for us, and you can travel back to Catfish Creek whenever you want, or fly your friends and family in."

She laughed, tears in her eyes. "Are you promising me the world?"

"Yes, you can have it all." He leaned in, sealing his mouth to hers, passionately, seductively taking control of the kiss. But as he backed away, he knew he wasn't done claiming her.

ROCK STAR

"Watch the cat," he called to one of the stagehands.

The brunette frowned but started to make her way over.

Before Rae could object, Travis took her hand and tugged hard, leaving her no choice but to follow him onto the stage. He felt her dragging her feet, but there was no stopping him, not now. And when the crowd caught sight of them and began roaring in excitement, he smiled.

Once he reached the microphone, he turned back to her and chuckled at finding her hand over her eyes, obviously embarrassed at being the focus of thousands of people. He squeezed her hand, and she lowered her other one, giving him quite the cute glare and smile combo. He turned to the mic and said, "New York, I'd like you to meet Rae Evans."

Thunderous applause echoed throughout the stadium.

"Oh, God," Rae mouthed, placing her hand over her lips.

Before she could stop him, Travis dropped her hand, leaving her there for a moment, and moved toward his guitar case near his drummer. As he passed, the guys in his band all grinned at him, obviously knowing by the times he'd talked about her that she was the muse behind all his song lyrics.

When he reached his guitar case, he took out what he'd placed in there after he made his first big paycheck. Rae had her goals that kept her focused on her dreams. He'd carried something with him for years to guide him. When he moved to her again, she looked half ready to kick his ass for leaving her alone and partly ready to curl in on herself.

He moved to her, wrapped an arm around her, and said into the mic, "You see, New York, this is my girl right here."

The crowd roared again.

"But I don't want her to be my girl," he said, watching Rae's eyes widen as he took a step back. Her mouthed formed a perfect O, as he added, "I want her to be my wife."

He paused as the crowd went wild, and he grabbed the mic and waited for them to quiet again before facing her completely and adding, "I've waited ten years to have you with me. I won't wait any longer. I want it to be us. I want you to be mine, and I want the world to know it." He got down on one knee, took the ring off his pinky finger, and held it up to her. "Let's not waste another day. I've carried this ring with me for long enough. But it belongs to you, meant to be on your finger. Marry me, Rae."

She finally looked away from the ring to him and smiled warmly. Her mouth moved, but he couldn't hear her over the roar of the crowd—though he didn't need to. He saw everything he needed to see in her eyes. The happiness. The love. He saw *forever*.

Overwhelmed, he rose, grabbed her, and kissed her for all to see, meshing the two parts of his soul into one. His kiss was hot, probably not appropriate for a crowd, and would be all over social media tomorrow. Good. He wanted the world to see what she did to him.

When he leaned away, he returned the mic to the stand and moved away, keeping what he said next private. He brushed the tears from her face, and he knew one thing for certain. Life had never been better than at this moment. "Saying I love you really doesn't seem to encapsulate what I feel," he said to her. "But I do, Rae. God, I love you so much."

"And I love you." She smiled, and surprising him, she asked, "But I need you to make me a promise, okay?"

"Anything," he declared.

She got right close to him and gave a sweet smile. "Promise to always kiss me under the moonlight and love me 'til the sun comes up."

"You remembered?" he said, brushing his thumbs across her damp cheeks.

"I could never forget." She smiled. "But there's something else we really need to do right now that's of the utmost importance."

"What's that?"

She glanced behind her, and when he followed her gaze, he saw Harry swatting at the stagehand attempting to pet him. Rae turned back and laughed. "We need to get Harry out of his crate, or he's going to hate you forever. And believe me, you'll live to regret ever making him angry."

And that's when Travis knew, life would never be the same again.

It'd be better.

EPILOGUE

Two years and three days later…

traviswalker ⊘   Follow

♥ **1.7m likes** 💬 **76.1k comments**
She's the best thing I've ever created. To the most beautiful mama
in the world, Rae…I love you!

ACKNOWLEDGMENTS

Much love to my family; my readers, my editor, Christa, my copy editor, Chelle, my assistant, Michelle, the kick-ass authors in my sprint group, and my cover photographer, Sara, and my cover designer, Charity. This book couldn't have happened without all of you! To Carrie Ann Ryan for coming up with this kick-ass idea, thank you for asking me to be a part of the Bad Boy Homecoming world. To Kennedy Layne, Katee Robert, and Avery Flynn, thanks for being the absolute coolest authors ever through this project. I adore you all!

A BAD BOY HOMECOMING

Thank you so much for reading **Rock Star**! Travis and Rae's story is part of the fun and sexy **Bad Boy Homecoming** series. Each book is a complete standalone but we hope you'll go through each of the romances to see your favorite characters make special appearances and see just how the reunion went down. Each book carries at least one of our favorite tropes as well as a few high school flashbacks that make us smile and shake our heads. If you enjoyed the book, we'd love if you could please leave a review to show us how much. Reviews help authors every day and we totally appreciate it.

Thank you for coming to the Bad Boy Homecoming reunion and we hope you'll not only find a romance you love, but a few authors as well.

Happy Reading!

The Books of Bad Boy Homecoming
Dropout by Carrie Ann Ryan
Trouble by Avery Flynn
Prom Queen by Katee Robert
Honor by Kennedy Layne
Rock Star Stacey Kennedy

BY STACEY KENNEDY

Single Titles

Five-Alarm Masquerade (anthology, Hot Shots)

Rock Star (Bad Boys Homecoming)

Filthy Dirty Love

Heartbreaker

Skirt Chaser (coming soon)

Dirty Little Secrets

Bound Beneath His Pain

Tied to His Betrayal

Restrained Under His Duty

Cuffed by His Charm (coming soon)

Club Sin

Claimed

Bared

Desired

Freed

Tamed

Commanded

Mine

Stay up-to-date with Stacey's new releases by visiting these links:

Stacey's Newsletter
Staceykennedy.com/newsletter

Website
Staceykennedy.com

Facebook
Facebook.com/authorstaceykennedy

Instagram
Instagram.com/staceykennedybooks

Twitter
@Stacey_Kennedy

USA Today bestselling author Stacey Kennedy has written more than 30 romances, including titles in her wildly hot Club Sin, Dirty Little Secrets, and Filthy Dirty Love series. Her books are about real people with real-life problems, searching for that special thing we call love...in a very sexy way. When she's not burning up the pages and setting e-readers ablaze, she's living her happily ever after with her husband and two young children in southwestern Ontario. She's a firm believer that wine, chocolate, and sinfully sexy books can cure all of life's problems. To keep in touch with Stacey, get updates right to your inbox at http://www.staceykennedy.com/newsletter/.

staceykennedy.com
Facebook.com/authorstaceykennedy
@Stacey_Kennedy

Want more Bad Boy Homecoming? Check out the next romance in our sexy reunion stand alone series:

DROPOUT

by CARRIE ANN RYAN

CHAPTER 1

Grayson Cleary wrapped his fingers around the lead pipe below him and grunted, annoyed it was taking this long to get the job done. He let out a breath, tightened his grip, and pulled. The pipe that some idiot had jammed underneath the carriage of the truck propped above him came out with a screech and almost banged him right on the head.

He let out a curse and rolled out from under the vehicle, flipping off his friend when Brody pressed his lips together as he held back a laugh.

"Did you hit yourself?" Brody asked, a little concern in his tone. At least the man had that. Now that he had a woman, he at least tried to act like he cared more than the others at their shop.

Grayson shook his head. "Came close, though." He held up the pipe. "Why did this guy think this would make his truck sound like it had a bigger engine? It literally did nothing except freeze the whole damn thing when he tried to go up a hill."

Brody shrugged, wiping his hands on one of the garage rags. "Saw it on YouTube, apparently."

Grayson pinched the bridge of his nose, a headache coming on fast, then remembered he still had engine grease and God knew what else on his hands and let out yet another curse. Thank fuck they weren't in the public part of the auto body and mechanic shop or Grayson probably would have been fired years ago. Cursing came naturally to him, and it had been a long time since he'd been in a position where he actually cared who heard the words coming out of his mouth.

Considering that his best friend Leah had an even dirtier mouth than he did, he figured it could always be worse.

"At least we don't have to clean up as many keyholes or fix dents in doors these days since that viral tennis ball video seems to have died down." Grayson went to the sink after dropping the pipe on the bench and washed his hands. He'd never fully get the grease out from under his fingernails—hazard of the job he loved—but he'd at least be cleaner than before.

"How many idiots broke their windows trying to push air into their keyhole?" Brody asked with a shake of his head. "I mean, it was good money for the shop, but still."

Grayson let out a breath and glanced at the clock above the work area, subtracting seven minutes and adding an hour. The damn thing had been off for four years now, but the owner liked to keep everyone on their toes. Now, doing the math to figure out the time without having to take out their phones—and potentially breaking them because of the grease—had become second nature. What it said about him that he'd rather do the math than find a ladder and fix the stupid thing he didn't know, but at least he wasn't the only one who just went with the flow.

"They're idiots for sure," he said absently. "I'm done for the day." He gestured to the truck still on the lift. "Rick wanted to do the oil change when he got in tomorrow. Once he does, I'll give it a once over and make sure the pipe didn't do any permanent damage."

Brody let out a breath. "I'm done too. And, yeah, I don't really want to think about what damage that DIY job might have cost this guy."

"His fault for following a dumbass video." Grayson cleaned up his area of the bench and wrote down a few notes for the next day as Brody did the same. "You want to get a beer before you head home."

Brody shook his head. "Can't. Holly's taking the night off from grading, so I'm taking her to dinner before we have sex on the new couch."

Grayson snorted as he grabbed his stuff. "She okay with you telling the world about your sex plans? Wait, you two really have sex plans?"

Brody smiled like a man who was not only in love but one

who got laid on a regular basis. "She likes lists, and I like making sure she can check things off. What can I say? Sex on the couch sounds fun, and if she can use a shiny sticker on her to-do list later after I make her come, then all the better."

Grayson would never understand couples in committed relationships. They were truly a weird and unregulated group of people. "Whatever you say, man."

"Maybe you can grab Leah and get a beer if you're thirsty." The man winked, and Grayson rolled his eyes.

"I'm not having sex with Leah. Never have. Never will." He shuddered just thinking about it.

"What? She's sexy. You have to admit that. And she's smart as hell. That's usually your type, right?" Brody slid on his light leather jacket since the man had driven his bike to work. It might be a little too warm for a coat, but Brody had promised his new girl that he'd be safe.

Grayson froze. "I wasn't aware I had a type." The fact that Brody had just described not only the last woman he'd slept with but also the first woman he'd ever wanted in his bed worried him. He didn't have a type, right? And it sure as hell wouldn't be *her*.

Grayson quickly pushed that visual out of his head. He *knew* why she kept invading his thoughts, and there was no way he wanted to go down that road again.

Brody raised a brow and snorted. "If that's what you want to keep telling yourself…"

DROPOUT

"Don't you have a couch to break in?"

"That I do, Grayson. That I do." The man by his side practically whistled. If Grayson didn't like him so much, he'd probably punch Brody right in the face just to keep him quiet. It wasn't that he was jealous of the clearly well-lubed man—okay, maybe he was a little jealous, but that wasn't all of it.

Grayson opened the door for them both as they went to the back lot where the employees were allowed to park. Their little shop had started picking up business recently, and Grayson had a feeling their employee lot would soon be no more. Not that he minded more business since that meant steady work, but he didn't like the idea of having to park way the hell away with snow on the ground. As Denver usually snowed overnight or in the morning before melting away in the afternoon and icing over, that meant Grayson would be stuck with a shitty space, no matter what he did.

"Drive safe," he called out to Brody as the other man swung his leg over his bike.

"You too. See you after the long weekend." And with that, the other man drove off, leaving Grayson standing by the side of his old truck that he'd done his best to remodel over the years. He could probably afford a new truck now, but he'd spent countless hours on his baby and didn't want to part with it. When he'd first bought it, he'd barely had two cents to his name, but he'd needed a vehicle to get to work. At the time, he had lived on canned green beans and whatever food Leah brought over when he couldn't afford groceries on his own. It wasn't easy to find jobs these days with just a high school education—and barely one at that when it came to him.

He slid into his truck and banged his head on the steering wheel a few times. He needed to get the past out of his head and start living again. Only it wasn't that easy when he had his best friend on his back about everything they'd done before they came to Denver—or rather, what they *hadn't* done.

Grayson drove home, blaring music from his high school days since that was now the *classic rock* station. Dear Lord, it had only been ten years, but that apparently meant a throwback in the music world. He desperately needed a beer. He pulled into his driveway, grabbed his things, and headed inside the small, two-bedroom home he'd bought with his blood and tears a year or so back. The bank might own most of the place, but he made his monthly payments so he could call something *his* rather than it being rented, borrowed, or stolen.

He wasn't that man anymore. Hadn't ever been if anyone bothered to look beneath the surface. But to those who had thought to know him back when, he'd been the dropout, the slacker, the quiet one in the back who hadn't done much with his life. They hadn't seen the kid who had to work two jobs to keep a roof over his head and go to school at the same time. They were blind to the kid who wanted to do more with his life but hadn't been given a chance.

Grayson twisted the top off his beer and chugged a good

half of it down, pissed off once again that his mind had gone in that direction. He might not have become a millionaire in the past ten years, but he'd made himself a better man. Why the hell did he keep kicking himself because of it?

His phone buzzed, and he picked it up off the counter, rolling his eyes as he read the screen. He didn't want to answer, but he had a feeling she'd kick his ass if he didn't. And since he wasn't sure he could actually take her—at least most days—he pressed *Accept*.

"What do you want, Leah?" He took a sip of his beer, needing the strength. He and Leah had been best friends in high school and remained that way after they moved from Catfish Creek, Texas to Denver, Colorado.

"I love that you answer the phone that way now," she said dryly. "I mean, it makes me all aflutter."

"Just get on with it since you call me at the same time every day to hassle me about the same damn thing."

"And yet, you answer your phone. It's as if you're scared of me."

He was. "I'm just being polite," he lied.

"You love me," she teased.

"Only on Wednesdays, and only because you saw me naked that one time and didn't laugh." It was their old joke, yet he knew if he actually said he loved her like his best friend and family, she wouldn't laugh at him. But making fun of it was always easier for both of them.

"We were like fourteen, and you saw me naked too."

"And I didn't laugh."

"Of course, you didn't laugh. I'm perfection. Anyway, I'm calling because you need to get your ass down here."

Grayson pinched the bridge of his nose. "I'm not going, Leah. You can't make me."

"For the love of God, just get your ass down here and come to this reunion." There was something in her voice that worried him, and he leaned forward.

"What is it, Leah? Do you need me to go down there with you?"

"I'm fine, Grayson Cleary. No need to make me your damsel in distress."

He let out a breath. God forbid, Leah Camacho ever admit that she might need help with something. "Why do you want me to go to our ten-year reunion? You hated high school as much as I did. Why go back?"

"Because, Grayson." She didn't elaborate, and he blew out a breath. She wanted him there for a reason, and he had a feeling it was because *she* wanted to go to show the others that she wasn't the person she had been before. And if Leah needed him to go…he figured he'd have to go. She'd been his rock for most of his life, and he hoped it had been the same for her with him.

"I didn't RSVP in time," he said, trying one last time to get out of it, just in case.

"I did for you, months ago. So get your ass down here."

DROPOUT

And with that, she hung up, leaving Grayson alone in his kitchen, holding his phone in one hand and a near-empty beer bottle in the other.

Apparently, he was going to his ten-year reunion. He wasn't sure Catfish Creek was ready for their town troublemaker and dropout to return. Then again, it had never been ready for the two of them, why start now?

In some ways, Catfish Creek, Texas hadn't changed much in the ten years Grayson had been gone; but in other ways, he couldn't recognize it. The town was about three hours west of Dallas— yes, Texans measured distance in time rather than miles most days—and a typical small Texas town where football reigned supreme, and Friday nights were all about the game and where to make out or party afterward.

Grayson hadn't been part of that crew, but he'd been around enough to know what happened for *most* people who didn't have to work two jobs to keep a roof over their family's head.

The town still had its main drag that held many of the landmarks, but it had grown considerably since he left and his family had moved closer to Dallas for his mom's new job. The Grange—the local dance hall and watering hole—looked like it hadn't seen a new coat of paint on the outside since he left. But, Frank Dallas, the owner and former bull rider, usually cared more about the inside than what it looked like to strangers and passersby.

The Hamburger Shack still stood, though it looked like it had had a slight facelift in the past ten years. He'd gone there with Leah and his younger sisters a few times when he'd had the extra cash to spoil them since the Shack had the best greasy burgers and spicy fries this side of Abilene.

There were a few new buildings and wider streets that showed off the chain restaurants and shopping centers. And there were even a few new roads that looked like they went to some new neighborhoods. The town had grown in the time he'd been gone, but he wasn't all that surprised by that. Catfish Creek might have that small-town feel, but it had a couple of Christian Universities that brought in hordes of students, staff, and professors. And with that came other jobs and new families. Towns without something like that or a natural resource to work on slowly died while the rest of the world moved on.

So even though Grayson could see some familiar aspects of his childhood, Catfish Creek wasn't exactly as he remembered. And, honestly, he wasn't sure what to make of that.

Leah had booked him a room at the local hotel where some of the out-of-town alumni were staying. Most had families to come back to, but since his had moved on shortly after he sped out of town, he didn't have anyone local to stay with. He'd be sure to keep his credit card on file though since Leah had a tendency to want to pay for things for him given that she had a better income. Grayson was just pulling up to the hotel but hit a red light before he could turn. He rolled his eyes, remembering that this particular light always ran long, and he had a feeling at least that much hadn't changed in the past ten years.

He let out a breath when he noticed who stood in front of a tan building across the street. Of course, she would be the first person he saw as soon as he came back. He hadn't even gotten out of his car and stepped foot in the damn town and he'd seen her.

Kate Williamson.

Valedictorian of his class, all around brilliant and talented individual. Kate with the long, flowing, chestnut hair that seemed to shine even more now than it had back when he'd been lusting after her in high school. Of course, he was pretty sure she didn't even know his name. Their high school was big enough that they could play 5A ball, and their zoning restrictions had been restructured enough to make that happen. Hence why his below-poverty-level family could go to the same public school as the Williamsons and St. Daltons. As long as football was taken care of, everything else trailed behind.

His fingers tightened on the steering wheel as Kate walked into the building, closing the door behind her. He couldn't believe he still reacted like this with just the barest sight of her. She'd spoken to him a few times in his life, more than likely promptly forgetting who he was afterward. They hadn't run in the same circles, and yet he couldn't help his unwarranted reactions.

She'd been the first girl he crushed on, the only girl in high school that had ever made him smile outside of his and Leah's friendship. Nothing had ever come of it, of course. She'd been dating Jason St. Dalton throughout most of high school, and had been the straight-A student to his solid-C education, but his dreams had held much more possibilities.

And now, he felt like a grade-A loser and perhaps even a bit like a stalker for even *thinking* about her like he had back in the day…and even now.

Someone honked behind him, and he cursed, noting the now green light. He let his foot off the brake, hit the gas, and turned into the hotel parking lot. Five minutes into this event and he already wanted to turn around and drive back to Denver. He parked and turned off the engine, taking steady breaths. He'd taken the week off, though he hadn't wanted to, but his boss hadn't cared. Grayson *never* took time off since he needed all the income he could get, but between Brody and a couple of the other guys, they'd filled in for him easily. After all, he'd done the same for them countless times. He'd also decided to make the twelve-hour drive himself rather than fly down. Not only was it cheaper, but he also had time to get his head on straight and prepare for what he was about to do.

Of course, all of that planning had gone out the window as soon as he'd seen Kate. Apparently, old ghosts didn't fade away as they should.

DROPOUT

Grayson Cleary was the class of 2007's dropout, who wasn't quite a dropout. He'd gotten his diploma a few months after everyone else did, but he had done it through the mail since he'd left town as fast as he could.

"Enough." He shook his head and got out of his truck. Time to deal with this because Leah needed him, and then he could get out of town as quickly as possible. If he were lucky, no one would recognize him or even care that he was back. After all, he was just the town's degenerate, nothing important.

After he had gotten the key to his room, he threw his things inside the small king-bed single and made his way back to his truck. Leah had told him he needed to check in with the reunion committee to get his packet or some crap like that. Apparently, there were a few things going on throughout the week ahead of time, but he knew there was no way he'd be a part of those. He was supposed to meet Leah for a beer later at the Grange, but he knew that probably wouldn't happen either. He was exhausted from his drive that had started way too freaking early in the morning and just wanted to sleep.

For now, he drove toward the school, past the football field that seemed even larger than it had been, and parked in visitor parking. Grayson narrowed his eyes as he rubbed his jaw, a sharp pang radiating through his gums before becoming a dull ache.

Well, fuck. He'd been clenching his teeth the whole way down here—despite the views of Colorado—and he was pretty sure he'd cracked a crown.

Jesus Christ.

If he had to find a dentist in Catfish Creek on his way to a damn reunion he didn't even want to go to, Leah would owe him more than a beer. Hell, more than a keg.

Ignoring the pain in his jaw, he made his way into the main school building where the email Leah had forwarded him told him to go. School was out for the year, so it was at least quiet from the hustle and bustle, and free of teenage aggravation and angst.

Thankfully, there was a sign about checking in on the right, and he bypassed the principal's offices. Leah had visited there more than he had, but he still didn't want to go down that particular memory lane.

He froze when he recognized the woman standing behind the table marked for the reunion. She looked a little older than she had back in high school, but her makeup hid most of that. She still had her bleach-blonde hair, teased accordingly to the current styles, and smiled wildly at him.

Of course, Karly Stocker was in charge of the Reunion Committee. Who else would want to organize so many things at once? She was like a dictator in love with control.

"Hi there," she said with a bright smile. Her gaze traveled over his worn jeans and faded T-shirt that showcased the fact that he worked hard with his body day in and day out. He'd bulked up some since high school and had the abs to prove it, and from the way Karly studied him like a cat in cream, he assumed she liked what she saw.

He had a feeling a single shower wouldn't get the ick feeling off his skin, at least not anytime soon.

When her gaze went to his face, her eyes narrowed. "Grayson Cleary. I didn't think you'd actually show up."

He was going to kill Leah for this.

Slowly.

He cleared his throat. "I'm here."

She snorted. "A man of few words, as usual. I'm a little surprised the rest of the committee agreed to your invitation, but here we are. I mean, *most* people who will show up this week actually graduated." She giggled, and Grayson clenched his jaw. Blinding pain shocked his system, and he held back a curse. He did *not* want to go to a dentist, but it looked like he wasn't going to get what he wanted anytime soon.

"Got the invitation anyway."

She rolled back her shoulders. "Yeah, it seems you did. And Leah is registered, as well." Her eyes narrowed once again. "Did you two finally marry? Her last name is the same, but knowing her, she kept it after she got married. She's one of *those* women. Feminists." She spat the word like it was a bad thing to think women needed equal rights.

Typical Karly.

"Just friends. Like we were before."

She snorted sweetly, though there was nothing sweet about

it. "Sure, honey. Whatever you say." She looked through a stack of envelopes and handed one over. "Here's the schedule of events and things you'll need for the reunion. The Brisket BBQ is tonight if you want to make it." Her gaze traveled over his clothing again. "And remember, the actual reunion is a masquerade." She paused. "A gala with masks if you don't know what that means."

Once again, he ignored the pain as he clenched his jaw. "I saw the description in the email."

"Sure you did, honey. Just be sure to dress appropriately, or they won't let you in the door." She giggled again, and he just barely refrained from rolling his eyes.

"Thanks, Karly."

She waved him off, a giant diamond on her left hand. "Bye-bye, Grayson Cleary. I'm sure we'll be seeing you around."

The way she said it made him think she'd be texting everyone she knew—at least those who she thought might care—that he was back and as much of a loser as ever, just as soon as he turned his back.

It had been ten fucking years but, apparently, he was right back in high school again.

Filthy love and dirty deeds so hot, they'll consume you. Get lost in filthy, dirty love in this series of standalones.

Heart Breaker

Handcuffs aren't just part of their job in this sizzling new standalone romance by *USA Today* bestselling author, Stacey Kennedy.

Veteran cop, Maddox Hunt, is all about the job. Sure, there are women—lots of women, truth be told—but there's no one special. Until a one-night stand from his past, rookie Joss O'Neil is assigned to his division. Suddenly, all he can think about is her. The scent of her. The taste of her.

Fresh out of field training, Joss has thrown herself into her job, determined to kick-start her career. And while police work has its thrills, her gorgeous new boss is what really gets her pulse pounding. Too bad he's nothing but a distraction. Especially since he's as devastatingly handsome as she remembers, and his sexy smile arrests her heart.

Now that Joss is back in Maddox's life, he has a plan: satisfy her fantasies and fulfill his every dark desire. Nothing is off limits. Her pleasure is the endgame…but even the best-laid plans have a way of falling apart. Despite his best attempts to keep his distance and have things remain only about the pleasure, Maddox soon finds himself breaking the only law he's set for himself. Don't fall in love.

FIND OUT MORE IN *Heartbreaker*.

Stay up-to-date with Stacey's new releases and join the mailing list.

Dirty Little Secrets.
Everybody's got 'em . . .
especially the kind of men who have everything.

Check out the first book in Stacey Kennedy's
Dirty Little Secret series . . .

BOUND BENEATH HIS PAIN

The *USA Today* bestselling author of the Club Sin novels kicks off a deeply sensual new series by introducing readers to Micah, a man who takes what he wants—until he meets the one woman he needs.

Real estate mogul Micah Holt exerts absolute control over all aspects of his life. He keeps his dark side hidden away from the press, who will chase down any hint of scandal. He's always in command of his world, careful to expose his closely guarded secrets only to those he knows he can trust. Then Allie Bennett shakes his legendary discipline. She's beautiful, pure, untainted. But is Micah willing to sacrifice her innocence for his own selfish obsessions?

When that sexy smile makes her body burn, Allie tries with all her might to ignore it. For one thing, Micah's her new boss. For another, he's as complicated as he is devastatingly handsome. Still, Allie can only fight so much before she gives in to his dangerous games. She knows he's got dark secrets. But when she discovers the true depth of his pain, Allie must decide how far she's willing to go to light the way for love.

FIND OUT MORE IN **BOUND BENEATH HIS PAIN**.

Stay up-to-date with Stacey's new releases
and join the mailing list.